Silvia

Silvia

The Stockman's Slovak Mail Order Bride

Sweet Land of Liberty Brides

Book 3

LORENA DOVE

Printed in the United States of America

First printing, 2017

ISBN-13: 978-0-9964744-3-6
ISBN-10: 0-9964744-3-9

Published by Royal Glen Studios, LLC.
www.RoyalGlenStudios.com

Dedication

To Emil.

Preface

Silvia flees the rough streets of New York and heads to the west hoping for safety and dreaming of love. Can Dell, a handsome stockman and reformed fighter, win her heart if he must fight for it?

After the death of their parents, Silvia and her brother, Emil, are on their own -- until Silvia receives a highly improper proposal from a man she thought was her protector.

Dell Casey, a dashing, black-haired Irishman, is working to keep the Eagle River Ranch left to him by his uncle. He needs to both sell his horses at an upcoming stock sale, and find a wife or risk losing it all.

When Dell fights for his ranch, Silvia will have nothing more to do with him. When new violence threatens, can she forgive Dell for loving her more than keeping his promise to renounce fighting?

Thank you for letting me know through your emails, Facebook comments and reviews that my "little stories" bring you joy, laughter, tears and a word of encouragement! It's an honor to have such wonderful readers.

Enjoy your trip back to a simpler time,

Lorena Dove

~Author of inspirational western romance fiction

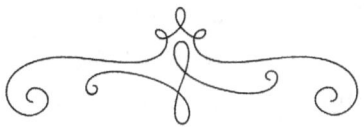

Chapter One

The small cot sagged just above Emil's head as Silvia carefully lowered herself. She whispered to him between the thin mattress and the metal crossbars: "Are you all right down there?"

"*Herr* "Yes, as happy as Juraj Jánošík himself!"

"Shhh!" Silvia hushed his gleeful laughter. "We're not outlaws, after all; I'm working for my bed, and nobody was using the space under it...."

"So I'm right," Emil said. "Juraj only took from the rich to give to the poor. You're taking up the riches of the bed, and giving the floor to poor me." He giggled.

Silvia couldn't help smiling to herself. Emil was so much like Da, always joking and laughing. But also quick to defend against any perceived slight to the family honor. Emil was already growing out of his third set of britches this year, and at 16, was almost as tall as she at 20. But so skinny.

Silvia hugged her arms around her shoulders for warmth and could feel her own bones pressing through her skin. It was one thing to hide him under her bed at night for a place to sleep, but sharing her meager food rations was turning them both into skin and bones.

"Tomorrow," he whispered from below, "I'll find a job. And if I don't, I'll be on the next train to Scranton. Uncle Stan says there's plenty of work making steel at Lackawanna for strong men like me."

"You'll do no such thing," Silvia whispered back in the darkness. "You'll find a job here, and we'll get a decent place together, like we had before."

"Ya, a decent place," Emil said, and tried to shake the image of the crowded tenement out of his mind. Even hiding on her bed at the

SILVIA

sewing factory to sleep at night, Emil had more air at night than he had in the cramped, dark rooms of the tenement. "You're my sister and I love you, but we both know I need to work."

"Yes..." Silvia's voice dropped off as she yawned. "You do. And you will, and we'll stay together."

Before daylight could break through the small smudged window, Emil was out from under his hiding place, down the long hallway and stairs, and out on the streets, well before the bell rang and the other girls rose to their work.

He loved the city first thing in the morning. No one was awake, and the gas lamps had gone out. The streets were a soft blue with lines of black and brown and gray where the buildings, doorways and windows towered over him. Within an hour, the first shopkeepers would be out sweeping their walks and opening their stalls, and he would be there to carry boxes or clean a floor for a bit of breakfast. He couldn't stand it that Silvia saved him half of her hard roll each morning. She was going to get sick, working long hours every day and hardly eating.

He passed by the store where Silvia used to work. That old Silas Jacobson can rot! Serves him right for running Silvia out of her job. He fantasized about showing the old man what it meant to treat people right. After Silas had taken over the old Luxe store, Silvia had no choice but to suffer under his harshness.

Eventually, Silas's son, Frederick, would run everything, and he was a different man than his father. But as long as old Silas was still alive, all Frederick could do was shield Silvia from the worst abuses.

When Silas demanded Silvia work till closing and then open the store the next morning for days on end, Frederick worked it out that she could have alternate Sundays off to rest. He often closed the store with her. Come to think of it, he'd been awful nice to them both.

It was good to be on the right side of a powerful man like Frederick Jacobson, Emil reasoned. His father wouldn't live forever, and Frederick would be in charge of everything. If only he could get Silvia to sweeten up to him a bit... but no. She said they were friends and that was all. She wasn't interested in Frederick after his father had tried to steal the inheritance of her friend, Nathalie.

Emil's loudly growling stomach drew his attention to the smell of freshly baked *kolache*. He took out a small whisk broom from his jacket pocket, and quickly went to work brushing off the dirt and grime from the windowsills of Laska's Bakery. He hoped if he worked quickly, Mrs. Laska would give him one of her delicious sweet rolls filled with poppy seed and walnuts.

"I see you're hard at work already, Emil." Mrs. Laska came out in the early light with a warm *kolach*, freshly dusted with powdered sugar, in a clean towel. "Have a bit of breakfast, but hurry on your way. Harvey says we have paid help and I can't be feeding every boy with a broom."

"Thank you!" Emil smiled at her. "I'm the hardest worker there is, if your husband could give me a chance."

"Time's are hard, and Harvey won't be hiring again anytime soon. I'm sorry." The older woman's smile was kind beneath tired eyes. "Come again tomorrow, why don't you? You can help me crack walnuts."

Emil nodded and hurried on his way, too eager to eat to continue in conversation. He ate his *kolach* strolling along, and when he had finished, licked the sticky sweetness off each finger.

Turning a corner, he nearly ran into Frederick and a young woman walking arm in arm. Her hair, if it were ever unwrapped from its tight bun might have been considered pretty, but her small eyes and perpetually pursed lips gave the impression of a nervous shrew.

"Hallo, Master Jacobson! Lovely morning, isn't it? And good morning to you, Miss ...?"

The shock on her face at being accosted on the street by a lumbering, emaciated, ragged boy changed to horror when Frederick actually greeting the lad.

"Good morning, Emil. Miss Gates, this young man is Emil Johnson, family of a devoted former employee of our stores."

"I see," Miss Gates said, and it was clear that she did.

Emil paid her no mind, but straightened his vest, stood as tall as he could, and stuck out his hand. "Any friend of Frederick's is a friend of mine!" She looked away quickly and perused the other side of the street. At her rebuff, Emil lifted his hand toward the sky and declared again the day to be fine.

"Quite so. Indeed," Frederick said. "Well, Miss Gates and I have business with her father this morning. Give my regards to you sister." With a tip of his hat, he steered Miss Gates around Emil and they continued on their way to a waiting carriage.

Emil laughed at the expression he'd been able to goose out of Miss Gates. Thinking Silvia would have a good laugh over it, he continued on his way to see what other jobs he could find for money or food.

Chapter Two

ilvia knew Emil was gone without looking under the bed. If he was caught sleeping at the factory, she'd be fired, and for now, it was the only income they had. Silvia and Emil had only each other since Mother died, and Mother had never been the same after Da's death. It was only for him that she even came to America, and she would have returned to Slovakia if she could. In fact, Silvia had been saving her money from her old job at Jacobson's store for just that.

Silvia made her way in silence with the other girls to the shop floor. With no way to talk above the noise of the sewing machines, Silvia was prisoner to her thoughts. She sewed in the dim light of the factory floor, whose glazed glass windows kept the heat of the sun from making the room unbearable.

What they did to protect from the heat, they made worse for the seamstresses' eyes. No one could work for longer than a few years before being moved off the floor to the packing or receiving rooms. Then when their eyes recovered a bit, they'd opt for the piecework at the machines again. If you sewed fast and accurately, it was the only way to make any real money.

It wasn't Frederick's fault she had lost her job. He couldn't stop Silas from firing her, but he had helped her get a new position and a place to sleep at the sewing factory. She hated the work, but it was her only choice and she would make the best of it.

Mother had used up her ability to make the best of bad situations. She couldn't face life without hope of seeing the Old Country again. After Da died, she had refused to eat and nothing anyone could say stopped her from her slow disintegration toward death.

As much as Silvia missed her mother's kind smile, she hated her mother's weakness. She'd never marry a man who would make her do anything she wasn't 100 percent certain she wanted to do.

Da had put family honor above everything—even her mother's happiness. It would dishonor the family for his wife or children to question him. It would dishonor the family for him not to work—even if it meant leaving the village and all Mother's family behind to work in American coal mines.

And when it came to defending his honor, Branislav Jahoda wouldn't back down. The company men insisted on keeping his name Johnson in the books—that's how the clerk had written it down, and that was his new name as far as they were concerned. To keep his job, Da had swallowed his pride—the one and only time Silvia ever knew of—and kept his mouth shut.

But the jeers of his fellow workers at the mining camp were one thing. When he met one of them on the streets of New York, Da had to defend his honor in front of Mother. What Da considered an honorable fistfight turned into a brawl when the other man's friends came running.

Emil was knocked down in the melee, and Silvia had dragged them away, her mother crying for her Da as the men beat him unconscious. He lingered for a few days, her mother tending his swollen face and knuckles, even as he continued to cough up blood. He died during the third night on Emil's watch.

Silvia sighed, crouching over the rough wool she was sewing into a man's coat. Piles of cut fabric lay next to her on one side, and finished pieces on the other. The woman next to her picked up the pieces Silvia finished and worked on the sleeve or collar, depending on the style. Silvia's job was to sew the long seams of the jacket backs and sides together.

A rough bump from behind didn't break her concentration. It was only when the foreman fairly shouted in her ear that she heard him. She stopped her machine and looked into his growling, mustachioed face.

"Are you Silvia? You're wanted upstairs!" He shook his head in the direction of the balcony that overlooked the cavernous sewing room. A flight of metal stairs rose from one side, and in its center were the glass walls and doors of the manager's office. From there, he could inspect the workers and keep an eye on any theft or laziness.

"Me? Silvia? Are you sure?"

"That's the name. Get a move on, and don't be away from your machine for more than 10 minutes. Go!"

Silvia lowered the needle into her fabric to hold it in place and made her way to the metal stairs, a growing dread filling her empty stomach. The last time she was in a manager's office, she was being let go. She didn't know where she could find work or live if it happened again.

She knocked on the wooden door frame.

"Come in!"

She turned the knob and stood in the relative quiet, her ears ringing.

"Close the door! Who can think with that din out there?"

She closed the door and found herself face-to-face with Frederick Jacobson.

"Good morning, Miss Johnson," he said.

"Frederick! I mean, Mr. Jacobson. Good morning."

"Yes, you two know each other—so I've heard. Mr. Jacobson would like a word with you. I'll go check something and be back in five minutes."

The manager grabbed his bowler hat and stopped to look at Silvia before leaving. "No funny business! I run a reputable place here."

"What?" Silvia laughed at the remark after the manager had left. "Frederick, did you hear that? No funny business."

"Silvia, how are you? I saw Emil on the street today, and well, I thought of you and had to come see you."

"Thank goodness. Emil is looking for a job; can you help him?" Silvia looked up at Frederick.

He crossed to her and put both hands on her arms.

"You're nothing but skin and bones, but just as beautiful as ever." He reached forward as if to kiss her.

"Stop that! He's coming back!"

"Silvia, I don't care. I can't stand not seeing you at the store every day. I've got to have a closer look at you. Your eyes ... your soft hair ... your perfect lips."

Silvia blushed. Frederick had always made her feel good with his polite ways and sweet words, but she didn't believe that he had real feelings for her. A man in Frederick's position had no business marrying a poor shop girl. And now she was even lower than that. Yet he had provided for her when his father demanded she be fired. He had gotten her the seamstress job.

"I want you to be mine, Silvia. I'll take you away from this place. Just say the word."

She let him kiss her forehead then. If this was a real proposal, she didn't want him to think she wouldn't jump at the chance. His lips started to trail over her to temple.

"Frederick!" She pulled her face away. "Please, I haven't given you an answer."

"What answer do I need? Your beautiful smile has convinced me of your heart."

"You've surprised me and I must think ... there's someone..."

"Someone else? Who? What man has stolen you from me?"

Silvia laughed, thinking if only he knew she had meant Emil. Still, she liked the ravaged look on his face at the thought of her with someone else. He'd come against a lot of opposition if he wanted to marry her. A test of his love and devotion would steady her resolve also.

"Just a boy ..." Silvia said. "A man, really. Someone who also may propose."

"Propose? Now Silvia, I wasn't—" Frederick stammered.

The manager's boots clanged outside on the metal stairs. Frederick pulled away, a smile in his eyes. "I'll send for you, my darling. Believe me, no matter what you hear — I'll send for you!"

He was at the door as the manager came in, tipped his hat, and quickly vanished. Silvia stood staring after him.

"Well? Time's a wastin', girl! Get back downstairs. And consider this your lunch break!"

"Yes, sir!" Silvia hurried away, stomach growling but new hope warming her heart.

Chapter Three

Emil finished his odd jobs for the day and stopped at Mrs. Laska's for a bowl of soup.

"Will you be staying this time to eat, child?" she asked. "Mr. Laska needs a new ear to listen to his stories; mine's worn out!"

"No, I've got to take this to Silvia. She'll be off work soon." Emil had to time his arrival at the sewing factory just right. As soon as the bell rang, the women would rise from their machines and head to the dining hall. It was really just a large hallway with boards laid down over piles of empty fabric reels. But the women lined up quickly to get their meager meal.

As soon as the workroom emptied out, Emil stole in. He kept close to the overhead balcony, knowing it was less likely the manager would walk to the edge and peer straight down than out into the room. Silvia knew to get through the line and meet him here so they could share what food they had for the day.

He pulled up a crate and propped his back against the wall. Another crate served for a table as Emil put the soup pail on it and pulled a small bowl from his pocket. Two spoons came out of another pocket and the table was set. His stomach growled as he waited, and he was sorely tempted to take just one spoonful before Silvia arrived.

"Emil, what have you brought?"

"Soup again, my lady!" he whispered cheerfully.

"And I've got two rolls and a slice of cheese," Silvia offered. "I saved my roll from this morning."

"And I don't want you to do that!" Emil protested, as guilt washed over him at the memory of the delicious kolach he earned that morning. He vowed tomorrow he would save it for Silvia. She was always thinking of him.

They dug into their cooling soup and slurped happily for a few minutes. When their spoons clanked together in the bowl, they looked at each other and laughed.

"Look at us, like two pigs at the same trough!" Silvia laughed.

"Not pigs! I prefer to think of Uncle Stanley's wedding to Aunt Patsy. Remember the soup they ate together? Supposed to mean they'll have a happy marriage."

"Well, I'm not going to marry you, little Brother," Silvia said. But I soon may be getting married. And Frederick has promised to find a job for you, now that you're 16."

"Almost 17! And I get plenty of jobs for myself. You'll see; when I send for you from Pennsylvania, you'll be happy I went to work in the steel mill."

"I'll never be happy for that, after what happened to Da," Silvia said quietly. Their father had planned to bring them all to Scranton, but the humiliating way the mining company treated the workers made her suspicious. Silvia was determined they'd find work that didn't kill them.

"I've had another letter from Nathalie," Silvia said. "She's expecting a baby, and wants me to visit. Oh, I wish I could go to South Dakota! Can you imagine how exciting it would be?"

Emil nodded. He wanted to go anywhere other than New York.

"But," Silvia continued, "she thinks I'm still working at the store — in my last letter to her, I told her I'd been made a shift manager. I didn't want her to think badly of me for getting fired and ... I guess I got carried away."

"You should go," Emil said. "That's it! Just write and ask her if you can help at the store while she's in her confinement. Maybe she didn't want to ask, but now you have the perfect reason!"

"I suppose I could, but ..." Silvia fell quiet. She loved Emil, but he was a boy and also her little brother. She didn't confess matters of the heart to him. "Frederick says he will find a new situation for me soon."

"Frederick this, Frederick that!" Emil said. "I'd think you were sweet on him for all you talk about him. Frederick can't save you! His father hates you, and this job in a sweatshop is the best he could do for you! Besides, I saw him today ... and he wasn't alone."

"Oh?" Silvia said with an air of disinterest she did not feel. "With one of his assistants, I'm sure?"

"A pinched-up prissy one!" Emil said. He laughed. "All airs and no manners, as Mother would say. Looked as if she would pass out when Frederick greeted me! But I didn't care. Miss Gates was her name."

"I'm sure it's his business with whom he spends time," Silvia said stiffly. "Now get yourself upstairs before the women finish their supper. Can you make it in time? I'm going to wash up and write to Nathalie."

"Aye-aye, Captain!" Emil said and saluted her. She laughed at his happy smile. "I have to warn you, I won't be taking your orders much longer!" He ducked as she swatted at him, and disappeared silently up the back stairs to the sleeping rooms.

Nathalie took the pail, bowl and spoons to the wash basin and swished them around in the water. She poured clean water from the tap and splashed her face in it.

Frederick ... with Miss Gates. Silvia knew her as a customer of the store, and not one of Frederick's assistants. Her family owned one of the largest dry goods import companies in the city. It was just the kind of match old Silas would approve of to further his business connections. Just what kind of offer was Frederick making to her?

Chapter Four

"Mind if I share the view?"

The tall man seated on a stone overlooking the valley flinched at the sound of the unexpected voice, but his piercing blue eyes didn't waver from the scene spread out before him. "It's too pretty not to. Pull up a rock."

The southern trail was always deserted – exactly why Dell Casey had taken it. He hoped the other man wasn't looking for company.

The old cowboy swung down from his horse, removed the reins and bit from her mouth and turned her loose to graze. He picked out a rock to his liking a few yards from Dell, sat down, and commenced to keeping the peace.

Dell's horse, Marble, moved closer to greet the newcomer, her grey-blue coat and black mane and tail shining brightly next to the reddish roan of the old man's horse as they grazed together.

Dell spit out the piece of grass in his mouth and felt along beside him for another. He let his eyes glance sideways at the older man as he plucked a new blade and slipped it between his teeth.

The man couldn't have been more than 45, but he looked older than the hills. His dusty hat lay upside down in the grass where he'd pitched it. Long gray hair hung in tangles over his ears and from the back of his near-bald head. Bony fingers splayed at odd angles from his cracked knuckles, and his sinewy arms rested with dirty elbows on his knees.

"Thinking about a cup of coffee," the old man said. "Name's Harrison. Harrison Taggert."

"Ain't got any," Dell said. "I'm Dell Casey."

"Gonna boil up a pot." Harrison quietly went about gathering a few sticks and built a small teepee out of them. He fetched his tinder box from inside his pack, dug up a few pieces of moss and shook the dirt off them.

"I got a match," Dell said. The old man nodded and Dell tossed him the roll of matches.

Harrison carefully removed one from the tightly bound roll. He set the match head to the striker on his box, and blue and green sparks leapt from it. He held it to the tinder with a trembling hand, and dropped the burnt matchstick into the small fire.

The flames leapt up and caught to the small sticks above them. With a satisfied grunt, Harrison leaned back on his heels and started to throw the match roll back to Dell.

"Keep 'em. Got plenty more back at the ranch."

Harrison nodded and put the roll away with the tinder box. He poured some water from his canteen into a small pot, and scooped in two spoons of dark ground coffee.

The men went back to their silence. After a time, Harrison poured the thick brew into two tin cups. It was Dell's turn.

He got up, walked over to Harrison's fire and took the cup. He smiled at the old man, so pleased with himself and enjoying a sip of the hot brew. The simple things. A horse, a fire and a cup of coffee.

"Got all I need, right here," Harrison said, echoing Dell's thoughts. "No one to boss me, no woman to tame me, and no shortage of rabbit and deer for my rifle."

"How long have you been on the trail?"

"Aw, I don't rightly know. Let's see, ever since I lost my claim. Yep, done rode away and never looked back."

Dell considered the possibility. The ranch was bigger than any claim he'd worked, and it was all his – if he could keep it.

"You part Indian?" Harrison asked.

"Naw –" Dell laughed. "Irish. But I'm an American. My family came over from Ireland. My uncle came first, and made it all the way out here. I've got the ranch now, just about."

Harrison looked at him sharply. "You must be one of them Black Irish, then. Never seen one before."

Dell laughed again. His mother's coloring had certainly come through in his own. His raven-black hair and black beard framed his lightening blue eyes and blue-toned skin. He didn't look anything like his blond and red-headed brothers, that was true.

"Heard tell they've got a mighty temper when riled. Knew a few Irishmen who worked laying track. Drunkenest, fightenest fools I ever saw."

"Seems we all have to fight our way through this life," Dell said. "And I wouldn't deny a man his drink, though it doesn't come without its troubles to some."

"Hmmph," Harrison grunted.

The two men sipped their coffee and looked out over the prairie, across the slough and down to the river. The sun had sunk lower in the sky and the clouds at the horizon were turning a soft shade of orange and pink.

Dell would have to get back to the ranch before dark and see to the horses. He liked the old man's company and wished he could stay and camp out for the night.

"Reckon I need to head back soon." He made no move and Harrison made no sign that he'd heard him.

"I said, I reckon I need to head back."

"Suit yerself."

"You gonna camp out here tonight?"

"Could be." Harrison put down his cup. "What's it gonna take to keep it?"

"What, the match roll?"

"The ranch."

Dell shook his head and slowly blew out the air from his mouth.

"Huh. That much," Harrison said.

"It ain't money. It's – see, Uncle Julius had certain ways. He married and lost two wives. Neither one of them lived long enough to give him any children."

"That so."

"Yes. So he left the ranch to me – on a couple of conditions."

"Ain't it always the way."

"Don't know about that. But it is for me. I've got to keep up the ranch's reputation for raising the finest horses west of the Missouri."

"Don't seem like a problem to me. Kinda tough to do, but a good reputation is all a man's got at the end."

"It's a lot of work, and there are a lot of ranches claiming the same thing. But that isn't the problem. I love the work and the ranch."

Dell waited for Harrison to ask. They sat in silence, watching the sun slide lower in the sky towards the horizon.

Dell hadn't told anyone about the other condition of the will. Only he and Uncle Julius's lawyer knew.

"Ain't ya gonna ask?"

The old man chuckled quietly. "I never ask a man somethin' he ain't willin' to tell."

Dell considered that. He'd thought all day up on that hill how to get a wife by year's end. He knew it wouldn't be hard to meet women in the bigger town of Sioux Falls. But he had to stay on the ranch to get the horses ready for sale and keep them in the best condition. Even if he did get introduced to a woman, he had no time for courting. And he didn't want the kind of woman who was willing to marry before they had a chance to get to know each other enough to believe they could be true partners in life.

"I hope she'll be a pretty one," Harrison said. He started to chuckle again, and finally his shoulders shook as he guffawed with laughter.

"What the –? How'd you know it was a woman?"

"Ain't nothin' else that can drive a man to his lonesome when there's work to be done," Harrison said. He stopped laughing and looked straight at Dell.

"I just ain't got time to find a wife," Dell blurted out, and after that it seemed he couldn't stop. "Ma always said to marry for my heart if it was the only right thing I did. I can't disappoint her, God rest her soul. But Uncle Julius has given me the chance of a lifetime. If I can't marry within six months of his death, the ranch'll go to my cousin. And that man hates my guts. Ain't no way I could work for him."

He talked until full sundown. Harrison kept feeding small sticks into the fire to keep away the growing shadows. Finally Dell stopped. He still didn't know what to do.

"Only one thing to do, then," Harrison finally said.

"What? Tell me."

"Keep your eyes on the horizon and your feet on the ground. If she ain't around here now, you gotta look elsewhere until she comes into view. Working with them horses will be good for ya, but bring 'em in early to Sioux Falls. There's nothin' sayin' you can't bring 'em early before the auction. Give you a couple'a days in town to scout out the availables."

"Ha ha – darn, Harrison!" Dell laughed. "That's the best idea – I didn't think of that! Only thing is, I'll have to work night and day to get the horses ready early."

"I ain't stoppin' ya."

"Of course you aren't. But what would you think about helping me? If it fit your schedule, that is."

"Ain't had a schedule in 2 years," Harrison said slowly. He smiled. "Where'd you say this ranch of yours is at?"

Chapter Five

His mind made up, Dell set to work immediately to get the horses ready for the trip to Sioux Falls. The stock sale was two weeks away, and if he could leave in a day or two, he'd have a full week in town to find a wife before the pre-sale showings.

Harrison said he would show up, but Dell saw no sign of him yet. He needed the help, and liked the older man's ways. He finished his coffee and set the cup in the porcelain sink.

"Aren't you going to have breakfast this morning?" Mrs. Magillan asked as Dell headed for the kitchen door. "It's not proper to be rushing off like this hungry and when there's good food waiting."

"I'm sorry, Mrs. Magillan. My plans have changed and time is short for the next day or two. Leave my helping for Ralston; he'll be hungrier than usual with the work I have for him."

Mrs. Magillan turned her ample body toward the stove. She stirred the potatoes and onions in the large black skillet with extra vigor. "Seems as though a body could use a day off around here, instead of more work. Ever since Mr. Julius died, there's been no rest for the weary a' tall."

Dell hadn't grown up with cooks and housekeepers. He knew how to keep a crew of men happy — they liked the same things he did: Hard work, regular meals, cool water, a warm fire, and cards on Saturday night.

But now he'd have to learn what made the household tick. The ranch's large rooms didn't get dusted and swept by themselves, and he'd be expected to give parties and hold meetings for business partners and townspeople if he wanted to keep the reputation Uncle Julius had built as the finest ranch in South Dakota.

"I'll be leaving for Sioux Falls in a day or two, and you have my leave to go visit — who is it, your sister? You take whatever time you need."

"That's very kind of you! I wonder how her daughter is doing. You know, she's very pretty — would make a fine match to you, Mr. Casey! The two of them never did get along and I've got a mind to tell her ..."

Dell quietly closed the kitchen door behind him and left Mrs. Magillan to her ruminating. He did need to find a wife, but wasn't convinced a relative of Mrs. Magillan's would be his first choice.

In long strides, Dell crossed the kitchen garden, opened the gate and made his way to the barn. Uncle Julius had started with a shed or two and gradually built a large barn to accommodate the growing ranch. The large, grey structure had one set of doors facing the range and the other into the paddock. Stored hay needed to feed the animals filled its cavernous loft. The grain stores were lined up in dry bins on the lower level, and the carts, horse carriage and new hay cutting machinery took up one side of the main floor.

Dell opened the single side door and stepped into the tack room and the cool quiet that was the barn in morning light. Saddles lined the walls and the smell of warm leather and hay filled his nostrils. A desk, chair and lamp sat in the corner where he had placed them as his makeshift office. He wasn't yet ready to take his place in Uncle Julius's office on the main floor of the house. Didn't feel right until things were settled.

He dropped his hat on the desk and continued on to the stalls. Walking down the center aisle, he patted the nose or spoke to each of the two-year-olds, the four of whom he hoped to sell. The yearlings came after, then the mares. He'd helped Uncle Julius pick them five years ago when he arrived with nothing but the shirt on his back and a letter from his mother telling Julius who he was.

The mares were good-sized and stout for quarter horses. They had good bones, even temperaments and most important, cow sense. They could pull a carriage or work a herd with the same ease.

They'd lost one of the mares over the winter when she foaled too early. He had found her and her half-born foal out on the range. Dell closed his eyes and crossed his heart at the memory. He couldn't afford to keep any of the two-year-olds, but one of the yearling fillies looked like she'd make a good replacement as a dam.

"There now, good mornin', feeding time's coming," he crooned as he went down the line, stopping before the last stall. "And now, Marble, how are you this fine morning?"

The beautiful blue roan whinnied and nuzzled her nose into Dell's hair. He hugged and patted her smooth neck and ran his hands through her black mane. "That's right, I love you, too," he whispered.

"Pshaw! It comes to nothin', lovin' on the stock like that!"

"What would you know about horses, then?" Dell replied, not bothering to take his attention from Marble.

"A heck of a lot more than you, that's for sure!" Ralston answered. "You'll find out once the ranch becomes mine, I reckon. Heard Uncle Julius left an impossible task for ya to complete the deal."

Dell whipped around to face his cousin. Ralston's wiry frame flinched briefly before he turned and spit on the floor.

"It ain't impossible," Dell said, his eyes flashing. "It's just —"

"Hopeless. Yeah, very." Ralston snorted and went to dip the scoop in the grain bins. "There ain't a woman you'd marry for miles. I'll be the rightful owner here when your time's up. First thing I'll do is sell that blue roan. She'll fetch a pretty penny."

Dell opened his mouth to reply, but had to admit Ralston was right. There wasn't a woman in miles for him ... but maybe he could find one in Sioux Falls.

He hated to leave the horses in Ralston's care, but for the time being Ralston worked for him and would do what he said. He had to get to town for supplies if he was going to be ready to leave in two days. Harrison's plan was a good one, and with any luck, in two weeks he'd return with money, a wife, and the ranch secured.

Then he'd kick Ralston out on his own and never have to see his simpering face again.

He got the saddle from the tack room and put it on Marble while she ate. He the tightened the cinch gently around her growing belly.

He'd ride her to town, but in her condition, he couldn't chance taking her to Sioux Falls. She hadn't foaled in two years, and he almost had given up thinking she could. But after the other mares delivered this spring, it turned out Marble was carrying for a later delivery. She was eager to work and needed the exercise, so the two rode off without another word to Ralston.

Chapter Six

ell rode into town and up to the general store. He tied off Marble and strode up the wooden steps and into the store.

At the sound of the bell jingling, Nathalie Maduro looked up from her books at the counter and smiled.

"Dell Casey, you're out and about mighty early," she said.

"Yes, ma'am. Have to get supplies for my trip to Sioux Falls day after tomorrow."

"So soon? I thought the horse auction was in two weeks."

"It is, yes, but I'm going spend a few days there in advance looking for a – looking for buyers. Would like my horses to go to good owners." Dell recovered a bit, but Nathalie raised an eyebrow.

"There's a lot to do in the city. I'm sure you'll meet a lot of – buyers," she said slowly. "Now, what can I get for you?"

Nathalie came out from around the counter, her gait slow and waddling a bit as she negotiated the small space. She pressed one hand into the small of her back as she stood in front of Dell.

Dell was comfortable around expectant animals, but he looked down in embarrassment at the sight of the glowing mother-to-be in front of him. "Aw, Miss Nathalie, I can get it myself. Wouldn't want to trouble you in your condition."

"Nonsense! I'm as healthy as a horse!" Nathalie said, laughing.

Dell chuckled with her. "All right then, I've got my list right here. You just point it out to me, and I'll do the reachin' and haulin'. Don't you have any help today?"

"Not this early," Nathalie said. "Isadore's away on a case, and Peter's coming in a bit later so he can stay and close up for me. I'm hoping to find another assistant soon, before I'm too fat to get in and out behind the counter!"

"Miss Nathalie, you're not fat. A woman in your condition is downright beautiful, if you ask me."

"Dell! You do surprise me. I thought your mind was only ever on horses and the ranch."

"Yes, mostly it is and has been. But since we're alone, I've got to ask you something. It's personal. And private."

"I see. Mind if I sit, then?" Nathalie perched on a stool in front of the counter.

"It's like this. I need an introduction. Maybe a couple of them. To a woman. An eligible one."

"Hmmm."

"The ranch depends on it! If I don't marry before the end of the year, Uncle Julius's will leaves everything to the next in line. And that would be Ralston Jones. I couldn't abide it. He'll run the place into the ground."

Nathalie nodded. "What kind of woman, Dell? Have you ever been sweet on anyone?"

"Can't say that I have, really. Oh, I like to look, no use denying it. And I'm an OK dancer and enjoy my share of social times. But when it comes down to it, all the prattle and small talk it takes to get to know a girl just makes – well, it just makes my head hurt. Horses, I know. They talk with their eyes, see?"

"I've noticed, but I'm not really close to animals the way you are."

"They do. And they make sounds and stamp and well—you can just tell how they're feeling. Not like women. I've seen them smiling at me one second and up and burst into tears the next."

Nathalie had to laugh. "Yes, we do that sometimes!"

"It's downright confusing! I'd like a woman, a wife, who I could figure out just a little bit. Maybe part of the time."

"Well, you'll have to talk to Isadore about that. He says the entire U.S. Code is less jumbled and confusing than the female mind."

"If you think of anyone, I'd be much obliged to meet her," Dell said. "Maybe I'll find who I'm looking for in Sioux Falls."

"I do know of someone ..." The bell at the door stopped Nathalie from finishing her thought.

"Good morning, thank goodness you're here, Nathalie!" Mrs. Simms came barging in, followed by her daughter, Allison.

"Good morning, Mrs. Simms." Nathalie stood. Dell shifted on his feet and disappeared down an aisle.

"Good morning, Nathalie," said Allison. "Mother, can't you see Nathalie and Mr. Casey were talking?"

"It's all right, we're finished for now," Nathalie said. "How can I help you?"

Mrs. Simms rattled on about her current crisis of finding the right material for a new dress for Allison. A dance was being held and her daughter simply had to have a new dress in time.

Allison looked around the store for Peter. Her face fell when she didn't find him.

"He'll be here before supper," Nathalie whispered to her.

Allison smiled as her face blushed pink. "Is it that obvious?"

"To me, yes," Nathalie said.

"Why Mr. Casey, won't you come and look at this material with me? I need a man's opinion on which color best compliments Allison's lovely complexion!"

"Mother!"

"It's all right, Allison, come stand here in the light." Mrs. Simms held up part of a bolt of cloth in front of her daughter. "What do you think, Mr. Casey? The blue gingham?"

"Well ... I ... uh ..." Dell stammered.

"...Or this pink calico?" Mrs. Simms switched to the different fabric.

Allison's cheeks turned from bright pink to a warm red. "Really, Mother! I'm sure Mr. Casey has more important things to do."

Dell stopped listening to Mrs. Simms and took a long look at Allison. Her blonde hair hung past her shoulders, with the sides pulled back revealing delicate cheekbones and small ears. She couldn't have been more than 19, maybe 20, he thought. A bit young, but she was pleasant to look at and he liked that she didn't want a fuss made over her.

"I think any dress would look pretty on you," he said. "But I think the blue check goes right nice with your hair."

"The gingham it is, then!" Mrs. Simms cried triumphantly. "I'll need 10 yards, please Nathalie. Allison, carry the bolt for her to the counter."

Allison reached for the material but Dell stepped in front of her. "Allow me," he said, and shifted the sack of coffee in his hand to reach for the fabric bolt with his right. He pulled it out of its place and put it on his shoulder to carry it to the front.

"Thank you, Mr. Casey," Allison said. Her mother looked at her with a big smile, but Allison shook her head and rolled her eyes. Mrs. Simms smacked her lightly on the arm.

"You could do worse!"

Dell paid for his coffee, rope and other supplies before Nathalie set to measuring the fabric. "Thank you. I hope I didn't trouble you with my talk earlier."

"Not at all, Dell. I wish you best of luck in Sioux Falls, that you find good buyers. But promise me you'll wait till you get back before you make any other ... final decisions."

Dell cocked his head toward Allison. "Are you thinking what I'm thinking?"

Nathalie smiled. "I don't think so, no. Just give me a little time and you may find your dilemma solved when you return."

As soon as Dell, Mrs. Simms and Allison left, Nathalie sat down to write again to Silvia.

Dear Silvia,

I'm glad you and Emil are getting along well. I was hoping after my last letter you'd consider coming out and working for me for a while, to help out until after I have the baby. But now I have something more to tell you.

A prominent man in our area, Dell Casey, is looking for an introduction to a woman that could become his wife. He's heir to one of the best horse ranches in the state, and needs to be married to fulfill the terms of the will. Silvia, when talking to him, I immediately thought of you. He's a plain-spoken man and wants a woman who is honest and easy to understand. Not complicated or too full of herself.

Ever since I've known you, you always think of others first. You helped me so much in the store, and after I lost everything before I came to South Dakota. I've always wanted to repay your friendship and feel, even though I'm asking you a favor to come help me through my confinement, you could have a fine future with a man like Dell Casey.

He used to be a bit rough around the edges. He started out chasing horse thieves for his uncle, and has been in his share of scrapes. But from what Isadore says, he's completely reformed. We've got a proper sheriff and ranger now to take care of criminals, and Dell's promised to leave the law enforcement to the courts.

I don't want lack of money to influence your decision, so I've included enough for train fare for you and Emil. If you decide not to come, please use it to help you back on your feet after the loss of your dear Mother and Da.

Your friend always,

Nathalie

Nathalie took some money from the drawer and slid it into an envelope with the letter. As soon as Peter arrived, she would take it to the postmaster at the train station. She only hoped Silvia would arrive before Mrs. Simms could wrangle Dell into marrying Allison.

Chapter Seven

Silvia stood up from her sewing machine and stretched, trying to ease the kink in her neck and back from bending over it all day. The other women chatted and lined up for the bathroom for their afternoon break. Silvia needed relief too, but wanted to finish writing to Nathalie.

She took the folded paper from her pocket and read over it, not even believing her own news. She told Nathalie about Frederick's impending proposal, and how she would soon be leaving the "store" to live as a proper lady as Frederick's wife. She remembered his insistence to wait for him, and that he would come for her. One phrase kept niggling at her mind, and stopped her from finishing the letter. Believe me, no matter what you hear. What had he meant by that?

Maybe it's better if I find out before sending this, she thought. She already felt bad enough that she had lied to Nathalie by saying she had been promoted. It was best to send the letter after she knew for certain she was engaged. She put the paper away and got in line behind the other women.

EMIL WALKED THE STREETS, head bowed with the weight of discouragement in his fruitless search for regular work. He was tired of hopping from one place of business to the next, getting rejections and finding fewer and fewer odd jobs to keep his continual hunger at bay. *It's time for me to make a break*, he thought. *There's work in Scranton. I'll go first and get settled, then send for Silvia.* His mind made up, Emil headed to the train station to look at the schedules.

He sat down with the paper on a bench and tried to make out the timetable. A page from a newspaper lay next to him, with a photo half folded over of a smiling woman. He looked at it absently until it dawned on him that he recognized her. Miss Gates.

He opened the paper to see Miss Gates staring solemnly into the camera, seated on an ornate chair before a wall papered in flowers. A man stood stoically behind her, one hand on her shoulder. Her right arm was bent at the elbow so that her hand covered his. A large diamond ring reflected light from the camera's flash.

Emil read the headline twice, shaking his head. "Engagement Announcement: Miss Amelia Gates to Mr. Frederick Jacobson." He stuffed the page in his pocket, and ran to the sewing factory to tell Silvia the news.

He showed Silvia the paper as soon as he found her. "Isn't it ridiculous?" Emil said as Silvia stood, dumbstruck, the paper trembling in her hands. "I've laughed the whole way here thinking of Frederick stuck with that priss for the rest of his life!"

Silvia just stared at the photo.

"Don't you think it's amusing? Silvia?"

"Amusing? No. But yes, someone in this photo is certainly ridiculous."

"Great leaping lizards, you're not upset are you? Over Frederick? I thought if you liked him, you would have been all smiles and giggles around him like the other girls. You never seemed to care much about him."

"N-no, I guess I didn't," Silvia said. Her mind raced to figure out what Frederick could possibly have been offering her when he said he would take her away—when he kissed her and called her beautiful.

"I'm sure he's made a fine match and his father is happy," she said. The noise of women talking started to rise from the hallway as they finished their dinner. "You better get upstairs, now—"

As Emil rose from his crate, a tall shadow crossed his face. He darted into the staircase and stood still to listen.

Frederick crossed the floor of the sewing room and found Silvia under the balcony.

"What are you doing here?" Silvia exclaimed.

"I had to see you; time is very short."

"Congratulations to you."

"What? So you've seen the announcement. That's why I had to come. Silvia, I had no choice. My father insisted I marry into the Gates family. But Amelia and I are not in love! We have a, uh ... an understanding."

"An understanding about what?" Silvia's anger rose and she was determined to keep Frederick on the spot.

"An understanding about our marriage. As long as we keep up appearances, she will look the other way. I must be with you, Silvia! I'll provide for you and you'll never want for anything. I have money here for your living arrangements. You can leave tonight with me and I'll make sure you're settled. After that, I'll be gone for two weeks on my honeymoon —"

Silvia slapped the hand Frederick had extended to her. "And then what? I'll be your kept woman living in sin with you? How dare you? I'd rather rot in this place then be second to your wife!" She turned her back to him. "Just leave — now! Leave me alone. I never want to see you again!"

Frederick put his hands on her shoulders, trying to turn her around, desperate to make her hear him out. "Silvia, I know it's a shock, but think about the life I can give you."

"Get your hands off me!"

Emil shot out of the staircase with a low roar. He raced past Silvia, fist raised toward Frederick's face.

"Emil, no!"

His fist connected with the taller man's jaw, knocking him back a step. Frederick swung out and Emil ducked, coming at him again from behind.

"Emil! Frederick! Stop it!"

Emil knocked the hat off Frederick's head. "I'll teach you to keep your hands off my sister!"

Frederick turned around slowly, rubbed his jaw. "Emil! I don't want to fight you. But this is a private matter between Silvia and me."

Emil was enraged. A feeling of power surged through his body as he saw the other man's weakness. Defending Silvia, defending his family, obliterated any other thought.

He struck again, a blow to the stomach. Frederick doubled over and Emil hit him with an uppercut to the chin. Frederick's head snapped up and he fell on one knee.

Emil waited, the energy of his anger drained out through his fists. He panted in the near-darkness. "I said: keep your hands off my sister."

Silvia ran to Frederick. "I'm sorry, Frederick! He's just a boy! He didn't mean it."

"I think he meant it very much." Frederick reached for his hat, arranged it on his head, and stiffly rose to his feet. His eyes shot daggers down at Emil, then he turned to Silvia.

"Come with me now, and I'll not press charges for this assault."

Silvia's breath caught in her throat. Go with him? Now? Emil glared at Frederick and shook his head slowly at Silvia. She thought of her Da, fighting to protect the family name. She thought of her mother's tears at agreeing to leave Slovakia to an uncertain future. She thought of never doing anything for a man she wasn't 100 percent in agreement on.

"Run!" she shouted.

Emil ran.

SILVIA MADE HER WAY TO HER ROOM and flopped her exhausted body down on the bed. Emil wasn't underneath it and hot tears flowed down her cheeks. She rolled into a tight ball and heard a crinkling of paper as she pulled her legs up tight. She reached down feeling for the source, and found a letter from Nathalie that had arrived.

She read it in the light of her lamp and felt the weight of the stack of bills Nathalie had sent. *Oh, Nathalie, how could you know I needed you right now?* She wasn't sure about this Dell person Nathalie mentioned, but she was 100 percent sure she had to leave New York right away.

Silvia tore up the unsent letter in her pocket. She pulled out her one bag and packed her clothes quickly. She had never yet worn her kroj, which her mother had made for her, except for the fittings. The large, puffed sleeves of the blouse were flattened now from being packed away. She fingered the elaborate embroidery on the vest and skirt, and held up the long sash that her mother tied into an enormous bow in back. It seemed silly to take this with her, but she couldn't bear to leave it behind.

She picked up the embroidery box and the apron she was working on before Mother passed. She traced her fingers across the small red and yellow stitches, smiling at the bright flowers and patterns.

Since she arrived at the factory, she hadn't been able to stitch at night after all day at the machines.

In South Dakota, in the light of sunny days, she would finish her wedding apron.

Chapter Eight

It seemed as if Silvia hadn't stopped crying since saying good-bye to Emil. She begged him to come to South Dakota with her, but his mind was made up.

"It's Scranton for me, Silvia," he had said. The months on the streets had toughened him, but since the moment his fist connected with Frederick's face, he knew what it felt like to be a man. And that meant taking responsibility for himself and building a future. With Frederick propositioning Silvia and threatening to have him arrested, the full weight of his tenuous position in life had crashed down on him. He could no longer afford to be the little boy making mischief and sweeping steps for a daily sweet roll.

Silvia clung to him as her train whistle blew. "Promise me you'll be careful!" she cried. "Work hard and write to me. And no fighting, please, Emil!"

"I'm more worried about you. You're the one who has the longer trip," Emil said. He patted her hair awkwardly, not used to comforting her with anything other than jokes. "I'll be with family. By the time Nathalie has her baby, I'll have a place and you can come back and live with me."

"Yes," Silvia sniffed and raised her head off his shoulder, marveling that he had grown just a hair taller than she already. She climbed the stairs to the train car and Emil handed her bag up to her. He took a few steps back and she burst into tears again as the train slowly pulled away. She had stood on the steps waving her handkerchief at Emil until she could no longer see his face.

She slept awkwardly through most of the trip, her body slumped against the window of the train. The rocking car overwhelmed what little strength she had and lulled her into merciful sleep. She woke for small meals and to refresh herself, then sunk back into her seat. On the fourth day, the conductor gently shook her awake.

"Coming up to Sioux Falls, ma'am," he said. "You'll be switching trains here and need to get ready to disembark."

Silvia thanked him and gathered herself together. She saw a dusty town in the distance as the train rolled into the station. She got off with a couple of other passengers and checked the schedule.

"You've got an hour and 20 minutes until the Silver Star comes through," the trainmaster said. "There's a café in town if you want something to eat, but watch yourself! Stockyard sale is this week and the town's full of ruffians," he groused.

Silvia set off down the wooden sidewalk. The street was full of horses and carts, with a carnival-like atmosphere as people waved in passing and stopped to talk to each other. She marveled at the open sky above, so bright and with no large buildings blocking out the sun.

The sun was hotter than anything she'd ever felt in New York. It beat down on her, and her small hat did nothing to shade her face or eyes. She wandered into a millinery shop where the friendly owner helped her pick out something more suitable. She laughed at the thought of wearing a straw hat. It would never do to wear in town! But this one was adorned with a pretty pink ribbon and some tasteful flowers.

"Visiting from back East?" the man said. "You'll fit in a lot quicker out here if you're wearing a more practical hat. It looks pretty on you."

Silvia nodded at her reflection in the mirror, and the man wrapped up the delicate silk bonnet she'd been wearing in a small paper wrapper.

"Thank you. Can you tell me where I might find a quick bite to eat?"

"Ma's Café is further down the street," he said. "Or the Occidental Hotel across the way has a saloon. Might not be fittin' for a young lady such as yourself with the stockmen in town."

"I don't have much time," Silvia said. "I'll just see if they can wrap me up something to take with me."

Silvia left the shop with her eyes and face nicely shaded under her new hat. She made her way carefully across the street, having to stop in the middle and wait for carts to pass. The doors to the saloon entrance of the hotel swung back and forth as a constant stream of men came and went. She quickly passed by and entered through the main lobby.

The two-story lobby was grand for such a small outpost city as Sioux Falls. Piano music, loud voices and female laughter glinted across the open space from the saloon as she crossed the marble floor to the front desk.

"We're all full, ma'am," the clerk said without looking up.

"I'm not looking for a room," Silvia said. "I'd like to get something to eat to take back on the train with me. Can you place an order with the kitchen?"

The clerk looked up at the young woman before him. "You're not from around here," he said. "Where's that accent from? Ain't heard anyone talk like you before."

"I'm passing through from New York City."

The man raised one eyebrow.

"And I'm originally from Bratislava."

The clerk looked at her impassively.

"It's a city in Slovakia, on the Danube River."

"Is that so? That's a new one. We get 'em all; seems like the whole of Europe will be livin' out West before long."

"I hardly think so," Silvia said. "It's not easy leaving your homeland and everything you've known to come to a new country." Silvia's voice trailed off as she thought of her mother's sorrow.

The man seemed to soften a bit. "You must be hungry, then. I'll order you up a roast beef sandwich and a drink. Best you'll find this side of the Mississippi."

He set down his pen and disappeared through the doorway to the saloon. Silvia stood quietly, until a set of voices growing louder than the crowd noise caught her attention. She walked closer to the saloon doorway and looked inside.

The dark, wood-paneled room was packed with men at every table and standing two-deep at the bar. The piano player in the corner kept up a steady stream of lively tunes, and ladies dressed in bright blue, green and red dresses rose up and down the far staircases. Going up, holding the hand of a man. Coming down, fanning themselves.

Silvia was mesmerized by their beautiful gowns, and shocked at the amount of skin exposed as the necklines plunged to expose their ample bosoms. She peered in more closely, just as the fight broke out.

Chapter Nine

ell sat in the saloon at a table with Harrison. He had left Ralston behind to care for Marble, the other mares, and the yearlings. He enjoyed Harrison's quiet company, and the man knew just about everyone at the stockyard. Already, he thought he'd be getting good offers for the horses on the day of the sale.

But Harrison's choice of establishments didn't help Dell much when it came to meeting available women. A whole week in town, money spent, and he hadn't met any women he'd want to buy an ice cream for, much less court. Seems the locals knew better than to allow their daughters out unaccompanied in town with so many strangers in for the sale.

A voice louder than the others caught his ear. "And we don't serve Indians in here!" The bartender shouted. "I said, you better leave!"

A small man with black hair stood his ground at the bar. A crowd formed around him, ready to jump into action if he gave any hint of not complying.

"Could be trouble," Harrison said. "Bottom's up." He swigged the rest of his drink and moved to stand.

"Wait —I think I know that one," Dell said.

"It ain't worth it, Dell. This town's itchin' for a good bar fight, and you need to be as far away from it as possible."

"Then I'll just take him out with us," Dell said.

Dell pushed his way through to the man's side. "Look here, now, Harry," Dell said to the bartender. "George is as thirsty as the rest of us, and his money's good. How are you, George? Best rope-man I've ever seen, ain't that right, Harry?"

"You might be right, mister," the bartender replied. "But we've got rules. If I let George here have a drink, who knows if he comes back with his friends? Management says no Indians, and I've got a job to keep."

"Well, I'm his friend, and I'm a paying customer, too," Dell said. "Now pour the drinks."

Two men stepped in closer from the crowd. "You must be Injun yerself, then, if you're a friend of his," the shorter man said. "Sure look like one, at least half, I'd say. I'm with Harry. Can't start something there'll be no end to."

Dell turned slowly, his blue eyes sparkling at the insult. "You going to say that to my face?" His arm shot out to block the punch the taller man was throwing at George. The short man grabbed a chair and swung it over his head, bringing it crashing down on Dell. He staggered and wiped the blood from his brow before charging the two men and knocking them both into a table.

Harrison grabbed Dell from behind. "It's not worth it, Dell! Let's get out of here!" They looked up to see the doors to the street blocked by most of the men in the saloon.

They turned toward the doorway to the hotel lobby, Dell pushing George in front of him.

"Look out!" rang out a woman's voice from the staircase. Dell ducked and felt the air from a bottle whizzing past his head. It glanced off the hat of a woman standing in the lobby, and he watched in horror as her small frame crumbled to the floor.

SILVIA WATCHED with growing disgust as the fight escalated, and drew back from the doorway when she saw a chair crash down on someone's head. Suddenly, the swarm of people seemed to charge at the door, and three of them ran into the lobby, one with blood streaming down the side of his face. A woman's voice called, "Look out!" and all went black....

Someone was hovering over her, removing her hat and brushing the hair back on her head ... "Da?" she whispered, "Da, is that you?" Blue eyes hovered over her in concern. Those are not Da's eyes, she thought before closing her own again.

"Is there a doctor in the house?" a voice said. She heard the desk clerk holler back to the saloon for a doctor, and a man came stumbling forward.

Silvia smelled liquored breath on her face as a pair of hands roughly felt the bump growing on her head. "No bleeding. Most likely she's just knocked silly," the voice said. "See? She's comin' around a bit already."

Silvia turned her head away from the putrid breath streaming over her.

"Who is she? Is anyone with her?" another voice said.

"She's waiting for a train," said the desk clerk. "I got some lunch for her..."

"Quick, man, check her ticket." Someone fumbled around and opened her handbag. "New York City to Sioux Falls, change to head on to Foley," the desk clerk said.

"My train..." Silvia whispered. "Nathalie..."

She felt herself lifted off the ground and then sun on her face. She bumped along with one arm around someone's neck and the other lying limply across her dress. She tried to kick to be let down but her legs wouldn't obey the thought.

"Just stay calm, Miss," said the voice. "I'm taking you back to your train. Harrison, here, will see you safely to Foley."

Silvia started to cry. "My head – ow, what happened? And where is my hat?"

"You got hit by a bottle thrown at me, ma'am. Those flowers took a bit of beating, but they softened the blow and, thank God, the bottle didn't break."

Silvia sniffled and tried not to cry. The bright sunlight hurt her eyes so she kept them closed.

"There, there, you'll be all right. Wipe your nose now with that hanky in your hand."

Silvia moved her fingers and felt the cloth against them. She lifted her hand to her face and wiped her nose and eyes.

They came into some shade and Silvia heard the train hissing and rumbling on the track. The man climbed into a car and deposited her gently in a seat. He knelt in front of her.

"I'd take you myself, but I can't leave my horses before the sale. Harrison will stay right with you."

Silvia's head was pounding and her stomach started to feel as if she would wretch any minute, but in the dimness of the car she tried opening her eyes again. A face swam before her, with thick, beautiful black hair and clear blues eyes looking at her from under furrowed black eyebrows. She started to speak, but the train jolted forward. The man stood, spoke some words to Harrison, and she fell into a deep sleep.

Chapter Ten

So it's true, sister!" Mrs. Simms said to Mrs. Magillan.

"I swear, I saw it with my own eyes," Mrs. Magillan said. "Mr. Casey is out of town, and I was just straightening up the desk of Mr. Julius, God rest his soul. Wasn't my fault I knocked the will onto the floor! Or that I had to pick it up, and my eyes just happened to see it."

"A codicil, you say."

"That's what it said: 'Codicil. This will is null and void if my heir, Dell Casey, cannot find a woman to marry by the end of the year following my death.' Those were the very words."

"How wonderful! Do you realize what this could mean for Allison?"

"I came to tell you right away for that very reason! She's a perfect match for Mr. Casey."

"Allison! Oh, Allison! Where is that girl when I need her?"

"HERE, TRY THE CHERRY," Peter said. He handed over the bag of candies to Allison as they sat behind the store.

"I love cherry, but I'm not done yet with the grape."

"Suit yourself. Why not take the bag with you? I can eat this stuff any time while I'm at work."

The store bell jingled inside the building. "Be right back," Peter said.

Allison followed him with her eyes as he slipped into the store. She sighed and picked up the bag of candy he had left behind, holding it in her hands. She hadn't noticed Peter much until a few months ago, but his soft, brown eyes and kind smile had won her heart. If only her mother would approve ...

"Allison, you better head back home," Peter said from the doorway. "Your mother's out front, and she's looking for you."

"Thanks! Can you keep her a minute until I get down the street?"

"Sure thing! I'll pick you up later for that buggy ride I promised. Will that be all right with you?"

"That'll be perfect! See you!" And Allison rushed off.

By the time her mother returned home, Allison was sitting in the parlor reading a book. "There you are! Have you been here all this time?"

"Why, no, Mother. I was asleep in my room until just a few minutes ago."

"My lands, child, I've been looking all over town for you! We must go for the final fitting of your new dress — the one that Mr. Casey picked out the blue gingham? He'll be back in town for the dance on Saturday, and it must be ready in time!"

"Why? I can always wear one of my other dresses."

"No! It must be the blue gingham! Mr. Casey is looking for a wife, dear, and from the way he looked at you the other day, I'd say you are under consideration!"

"But Peter has already asked me to the dance. I promised I'd go with him!"

"Nonsense! What's a young man like Peter compared to Dell Casey! I'm sorry to disappoint you, dear, but really a chance like this won't come along often!"

Allison stood and set the book down on the side table. "Mother, I won't have you pushing me on Mr. Casey. If he wants to dance with me on Saturday, he'll have to cut in. I can't say no to Peter and then have no one to escort me!"

"Hmmm. You're right about that, my girl. Very good thinking. It'll be up to me to make sure you get one dance with Mr. Casey. Then, my dear, it will be up to you to see that he dances with no one else the rest of the night!"

Allison let out a breath. She had made it past one hurdle — she could still go to the dance with Peter. She had no doubt she could make herself unlikeable enough to Dell Casey to ensure he would not ask her for another dance, much less to marry him.

Mrs. Magillan spoke up. "I think you're both forgetting something. I could use a little help around the ranch house. Mr. Casey won't mind if I bring on Allison."

"That's a wonderful idea! Come to the dress fitting with us, and then Allison can leave with you straight away. Allison? Pack your things." The two sisters chatted happily as they made ready to leave.

Allison cried as she packed. She had never been away from her mother before, and now she wouldn't be able to see Peter at the store. She hoped with all her heart Mr. Casey returned from Sioux Falls with a wife.

HARRISON KEPT WATCH over Silvia as the train chugged along on the last leg of her trip. Before leaving, Dell said he would send a telegraph to Nathalie to bring a doctor to the station.

The young woman next to him was asleep, but restless. Her brown hair hung in damp trails along her face and neck. She held her crushed hat in her lap.

As the train pulled up to the station, he saw a woman anxiously pacing and looking up at the windows. He tipped his hat to her and she ran to the car as it pulled to a stop.

"Miss ... Miss ..." Harrison shook Silvia. He stood and pulled her limp frame to her feet, and picked her up in his arms.

Silvia came to with Nathalie's tearful face coming into focus as she sat by her side. "Nathalie? Am I really here? Oh, my head aches so!"

"Silvia, my poor dear! You've had a bad bump on the head. Doctor says you'll be well in a day or two, though a headache may linger." Nathalie leaned forward and the two hugged tightly.

"I hardly remember — what happened? I got off the train and bought a new hat. I was in a hotel lobby, waiting for someone ... No! I was waiting for my lunch."

"Yes, dear. Harrison told me about the fight. He said Dell was only trying to help."

"Dell? Is that who was fighting?"

"Yes, Dell Casey, the man I told you about. Isadore said he hasn't gotten into any trouble in a few years, but —"

"Well he was certainly in the middle of trouble in Sioux Falls! If it weren't for Harrison, I might have been killed. He tended me and carried me to the train. Where is he?"

A dark figure stepped out of the shadow behind the door.

"Here, Ma'am."

Silvia smiled at him and looked at his shiny, bald forehead and into his dark, brown eyes. Her brow furrowed a bit at the memory of thick black hair and blue eyes that she had seen at the hotel.

"You? You're Harrison?"

"Afraid so."

"Just try to rest now," Nathalie said. "You're here and safe with me. Everything will be better in the morning."

Chapter Eleven

y morning, Silvia's head still throbbed as she struggled to sit up. She carefully put her feet on the floor and a wave of dizziness overtook her as she sat on the edge of the bed. She was tired, but more tired of waiting for her new life to begin. She stood and opened the door, hearing voices from the lower level of the house.

She carefully walked down the steps, through the parlor and into the kitchen. An older woman sat in a chair, and Nathalie had her back to the door. A friendly face looked up at her from the stove.

"How wonderful to see you!" Mr. Gadsen said. "I'm so sorry to hear of your accident."

"Mr. Gadsen," Silvia said, smiling. "I've missed you since you left New York."

"I've missed you and the city, too," Mr. Gadsen said. "I never thought I'd leave. But love can play tricks on you, even at my age." He smiled at the older woman.

"Please, come sit and have coffee, if you feel up to it," said Nathalie. "Mother, I'd like you to meet Silvia. Silvia, this is my mother-in-law, Mrs. Maduro — I mean, Mrs. Gadsen."

Mrs. Gadsen smiled but did not stand or offer her hand. Silvia saw the blank look in her clouded eyes and came over closer to her. She placed her hand on the woman's hand on the table.

"Very nice to meet you, Mrs. Gadsen. I've heard so much about you from Nathalie's letters! How wonderful that you and Mr. Gadsen are married!"

"The Lord brought Isadore our wonderful Nathalie," Mrs. Gadsen said. "And in his kindness, he found room for two hearts as old as ours to be united."

Mr. Gadsen served breakfast as the women talked. Silvia's stomach roiled at the smell of the eggs and bacon, but she dipped her toast into her coffee to soften it, and got some down that way.

"Where is Isadore? I've been dying to meet him," Silvia said.

"He's away trying a case in the next county. His last telegraph said it would be finished soon," said Nathalie. "I certainly hope so! He promised he'd be here when the baby is born."

"I'm anxious to help," Silvia said. "You have no idea how your letter arrived at the exact time I needed it."

"It's time to open the store," Nathalie said. "Why don't you come with me and you can tell me everything."

SILVIA FELT STRONGER over the next few days and learned Nathalie's procedures at the store very quickly. "It feels just like old times, as if we were still working at the Luxe store!" Silvia said. "Of course, it is a bit smaller," she said, smiling as she looked around the rustic mercantile.

"Definitely smaller! But it's ours, free and clear. Oh Silvia, I do hope you love it here.

After the baby is born, if you can stay for a few months, it will help so much. Mrs. Gadsen is willing, but I'm afraid she will have a hard time caring for a baby while I'm at work. And I can't put that on old Gadsen, either! He draws the line at becoming a nursemaid."

Silvia laughed. "I'll see, Nathalie. Emil hopes to have a place for us both in Pennsylvania in a few months' time. I know you'll understand if I want to be with my family. He's all I have left."

"Yes, I do," said Nathalie. "But you haven't met Dell Casey yet — at least not properly."

"I know all about him that I want to know," Silvia said, as the smile vanished from her face. "Settling your differences with your fists is what got Da in trouble his whole life. I'm afraid if I don't keep an eye on Emil, he'll follow the same path and get himself into trouble — or worse. No, I don't need another man who fights first and asks questions later to worry about."

"I'm not sure Dell's that kind of man," Nathalie said. "Isadore fights with words — that's what lawyers do. I fought for my business, to keep it out of the hands of Silas Jacobson. We all have to fight in some way."

"You may be right," Silvia said. "But, 'A soft answer turns away wrath.' I can't stand the type of man who can't control himself."

Chapter Twelve

ell counted the money in the stockyard office from the sale of his horses. He and Harrison then started on the ride back to Foley. Harrison had returned after dropping off Silvia, and the two of them had negotiated even better prices for the horses than he had hoped.

They left the crowded town behind and rode on through the prairie in silence.

"You sure have a way with words — or actually, with no words," Dell said. "Still can't believe you got that man to raise his bid at the last minute."

"First rule of negotiation: He who gives a price first, loses," Harrison answered with a shrug.

"How'd you get so good at this, anyway? I thought you were a farmer."

"Farmer's have to haggle. Everyone does. You have to be willing to walk away, or make the other man think so."

"Isn't that what you did, walk away from the claim?"

"Yes."

"Were you willing?"

"Nope."

"Going to tell me anymore about that?

"No."

Dell laughed and slapped Harrison on the shoulder. "All right, my silent friend. Just as long as you let me know before you give up on me. Come on, I'm anxious to get back to the ranch and check on Marble."

"Don't you think you better check on that poor girl? She got hit on the head, on account of your foolishness. I told you it was best to get out of there."

"I guess I ought to. And I owe an apology to Nathalie, too. Had no idea a friend of hers was traveling through."

"She's a quiet sort. I like that," Harrison said. "'Course she was passed out the whole way. She was right nice when she woke up, though."

A picture of Silvia's ashen face crossed Dell's mind. He rode along in silence as he thought of the soft white skin of her neck, and was ashamed of the rude bump he had caused that grew under her long, brown hair. He remembered the look of love in her eyes when she thought he was her Da, and how they had clouded over in confusion before she passed out again. She was light as a feather, and he would have carried her all the way to Foley if she had missed her train.

The town came before them in the distance, and Dell spurred on his horse with the vision of Silvia leading him on.

THE STORE WAS CROWDED with customers when Silvia saw him in the doorway. Their eyes met, and she felt a pull to the blueness of them, to the calm, cool confidence that emanated from Dell Casey.

She blushed and looked away, trying to keep her attention on the customer before her. But when she looked up, he was headed straight for her.

"Dell! You're back!" Nathalie exclaimed, and took him by the hand to bring to Silvia. "Mr. Dell Casey, I'd like you to meet my dearest friend, Silvia Johnson. But I believe you two already know each other."

"Good afternoon, ma'am," Dell said with his hat in his hand. "I'm glad to see you whole and hearty."

"Yes, well, no thanks to you, Mr. Casey," Silvia replied. She reached for the bump on her head. "I've got a little remembrance of you I carry with me."

"I sincerely apologize for that," he said. "If I'd have known you were in the hotel lobby, I surely wouldn't have come through that door."

"And what choice did you have, with that mob after you?" Silvia said coolly. "Fighting always comes to trouble. But maybe you're not aware of that fact."

As soon as Silvia said the words, she wished she could take them back. For some reason, Dell's apology brought out the scolding sister in her. In reality, her hands trembled at being so close to him.

He stood a head taller than she, and he carried his large frame with such grace on his well-muscled limbs that he moved like a much smaller man. His trousers and boots were dirty from the trail, but his voice was soft.

"You have every right to scold me," he said, his eyes twinkling at the words. "I hope to make it up to you, and then some."

Silvia's face softened as she looked into Dell's eyes.

"I suppose I can give you the chance."

"Of course you can! And you will!" said Nathalie.

"A-hem." Harrison cleared his throat. "Nice to see you well, Miss Silvia. Dell, we best be moving on to the ranch."

At Harrison's reminder, Dell reluctantly broke his gaze from Silvia's face.

"I need to place an order," Dell said.

"Silvia can take it down for you," said Nathalie. "And I'll have Peter get it together and bring it to the ranch, so you can be on your way."

"Much obliged, Nathalie," Dell said.

"Right this way, Mr. Casey." Silvia moved to an empty spot on the counter, glad to get some distance from Dell so she could think. She'd already seen the kind of man he was — someone who wasn't afraid to get into a fight — and that sort of man was out of the question for her.

Yet her heart would not stop racing, and she quickly picked up a pencil to steady her quivering hand.

He stood across the counter from her and gave her his order. Flour, sugar, eggs, coffee. As the list grew longer, she looked up from her writing with a questioning eye.

"Are you out of everything?" she asked with a smile.

Dell laughed. "No, I guess not. I've been away for 10 days and just figured I'd get the usual.

Dell's blue eyes shone with a brighter intensity and it seemed like he had made up his mind about something.

"Silvia — may I call you Silvia?"

Silvia nodded.

"I'd like to invite you to the ranch. Will you come with Peter to deliver this order?"

Silvia's mind screamed *"No!"* but her heart disagreed. She was amazed to hear the words that came out of her mouth.

"Yes, Dell. I will."

Chapter Thirteen

ell arrived at the ranch, exhausted from his long trip. Hel walked up the front porch as Harrison took the horses to the barn.

"Hello, Mrs. Magillan!" he called as he dropped his leather gloves and his hat on the front hall table, and walked through the rooms. "I'm back!"

"Mr. Casey, how wonderful! Was the auction a success?" Mrs. Magillan said, coming out from the kitchen. Allison followed from behind.

"It was! Got the best prices for the horses of any ranch. Had buyers lining up for the yearlings when they're ready, too."

Allison gave him a smile and a small wave of her hand.

"Allison? What are you doing here?"

"Aunt Beatrice offered me a position," Allison said. "I hope you don't mind."

"A position?" said Dell. "What's this, Mrs. Magillan?"

"We'll be needing the help," Mrs. Magillan said. "She's a quick learner and it's nice for me to have some company in the house for a change."

Dell smiled. "I suppose that can work out," he said, as Allison blushed and looked down. "I'm going to wash up. Where's Ralston? Have him meet me in Uncle Jules's office."

"I haven't seen him today," Mrs. Magillan said. "Funny, he usually comes right on time for breakfast."

"Never mind, then. I'll find him myself. After I get out of these clothes."

PETER FINISHED PILING THE SACKS and boxes in the cart for his round of deliveries. He was grateful for the chance to go see Allison at the Casey ranch. He called to Silvia that he was ready.

Silvia was glad to get out and see the surrounding countryside. She climbed up next to Peter, and they quietly rode on the main street out of town. They passed the train station, and the post office. They passed by two churches and the little school that stood on one corner, quiet now as the children were out for the summer.

Soon they were out in the plains. The rolling grass stretched out to the horizon, and Peter pointed out the names of the families who lived on the claims they passed. To Silvia, most of the houses were nothing more than a shack, but some had been added on to and become proper houses and farms.

Except for the great, vast expanse of land and sky, the small claims reminded her of Slovakia.

They pulled up to a side road with an iron signpost: Eagle River Ranch. Peter turned the horse down the lane, and they followed the road down to the river crossing.

"We're not going across that, are we?" Silvia cried. "Where's the bridge?"

"No bridge here yet," Peter said. "The river rises too much in the spring. It would just get washed out. Look, it's nice and low now, and calm. We'll make it just fine."

Peter guided the horse down to the edge of the water, and chucked twice to encourage it to cross. Silvia held on as the cart bounced over the rocky bottom, and let out a breath she didn't know she was holding when the horse started up the small incline on the other side.

They drove up to the ranch house and Peter hollered hello. Dell Casey came out on the porch.

Silvia adjusted her straw hat on her head and smiled. Dell stood on the steps of a large, low house, nothing like the small shacks she had seen on the way. He crossed the porch in two steps and walked quickly toward Peter's horse. Taking it expertly by the reins, he held it steady for Peter as he climbed down.

"Thanks, Dell," Peter said, and took the horse's reins from him. Dell walked over to Silvia and put out his hand.

"May I help you down?"

Silvia smiled, and took his hand. She jumped down from the cart and leaned a little into him. "Oh, I'm sorry! Must still be a little dizzy," she said.

Dell steadied her on her feet. "No trouble. Here, take my arm. Would you like to see Eagle River Ranch? I have some checking up to do."

"I'd be happy to; do you mind Peter?"

"No," said Peter. "I'll just drive around to the kitchen door and unload the cart. See you!"

Dell stood with Silvia in the front yard and swept his arm out across the fields. "This was nothing but prairie grass. My uncle first planted in wheat in order to prove up the claim. When I came five years ago, we started the horse ranching in earnest."

Dell and Silvia walked along to a small creek. "Oh, the flowers!" she said. Dell watched as she rushed about, picking wildflowers into a small bouquet.

"In the city, I could only afford to buy flowers every few weeks," Silvia said, her face gleaming. "I've missed growing them so much! My mother had a cutting garden in Slovakia. I used to help her every morning cut baskets of flowers."

"It must have been hard leaving," Dell said. "Why did you?"

"The fields were divided up smaller and smaller each year," Silvia said. "My father said he didn't have enough land to feed our family. He wanted a better life for himself, but even more so for my brother and me." Sylvia swallowed hard and closed her eyes to prevent the tears from flowing at the thought of Emil.

Dell moved a step closer, but stopped when Silvia opened her eyes and took a deep breath.

"One day, a man came to our village with a paper flyer of a company in America that was hiring workers. My father wanted to leave right away." Silvia's eyes hardened and Dell could sense her body bristle with deep anger.

"But it took him a few months to convince Mother."

"I'm glad he convinced her," Dell said. "And that you are here."

"It cost me everything!" Silvia said. "Da went to the mines in Pennsylvania to work, leaving Mother, Emil and me behind. He returned every three weeks, but his pride was broken! He said he owed more money to the company than when he started working. He wanted us to be together, but we couldn't afford to leave the city."

"I'm sorry," Dell said. He reached out his hand to her.

Silvia took it and felt his strength cheer her. She stood next to him, calming herself by smelling the flowers in her other hand.

"I've told you my plans for the ranch," Dell said softly. "What do you want?"

Silvia looked up at him, losing herself in his smiling blue eyes. "I want to live a good life, for Da. The one he brought me here for," she said.

Dell wanted nothing more than to give her that life. He never dreamed that in his desperate search for a wife, he would find a woman like Silvia.

He leaned forward to take her in his arms and make everything right in her world, when the sound of a faraway voice pierced the air between them.

"Dell!! Dell, come quick!" Peter shouted from across the field. "Harrison needs you in the barn! It's Marble!"

Chapter Fourteen

ell dropped Silvia's hand and set out on a run for the barn. Silvia followed, falling farther behind as his long legs sped him away.

Peter met her in the yard and took her around to the barn. They went inside and down to the last stall.

"Why didn't you come get me?" Dell was shouting at Harrison. "Look at her! Where is that blasted Ralston?"

"I figured you'd be out right behind me," Harrison said. "Once I saw the shape she was in, I couldn't leave her."

The beautiful grey-blue horse was moving restlessly around the stall. Silvia watched in amazement as the mare lay down, rolled on her back with her legs in the air, first one way, then the other. Agitated, she got up with great effort to her feet again.

"How long has she been doing this?" Dell asked.

"Since I moved her to the birthing stall," Harrison said. "Seen this before, Dell. She's trying to get the foal to turn."

Marble laid down again, this time too exhausted after her roll to get up. Dell fell to his knees next to Marble's head. The mare was covered in hay and muck and her breathing was shallow. Her stomach heaved as the foal inside her writhed and moved, getting ready to be born.

"Oh, the poor thing!" Silvia gasped.

"Peter, get some hot water from the kitchen," Dell commanded. "Silvia, can you come in? Hold her head? I've got to help Harrison."

Silvia nodded and stepped into the stall. Her shoes sunk in the muck and her steps made a sucking noise as she crept along the edge to Dell. She knelt down, lost her balance, and fell onto her rump in the dirty hay.

"Come closer," Dell said.

She wriggled forward and Dell placed the horse's head on her lap.

"Talk to her," he ordered.

Silvia's heart pounded. The horse's large teeth showed as her tongue lolled out. Silvia marveled at the animal's black eyelashes and jet black mane. She began to stroke her mane and forelock, saying, "Shh...shh..." over and over. Marble's eyelashes batted at her before her eyes rolled up.

"Dell! Her eyes!"

"This is it," Harrison said. "Foal should be comin'. But there ain't no water broke. Something's wrong."

"The foal's still breech, then," Dell said. "Let me in closer; I'll have to turn it."

Silvia watched as Dell stripped off his outer shirt and washed his arms in the trough. He pulled up the horse's tail and reached inside. She couldn't look.

"I can feel the foal," Dell said, removing his arm. "Harrison, get her up."

Harrison came to Marble's head and coaxed the horse into standing. A trickle of water ran out of her.

"I nicked the sac, but the foal's rump is in the way. I've got to get to its legs and bring it out that way."

Harrison gave Marble's halter to Silvia. "Just keep her calm," he said. "If she senses you're afraid, it'll just make it harder for her – and all of us."

Silvia nodded and hung on to Marble's neck with the horse's head over her shoulder.

"All right. I'm going in for it. Harrison, get a rope ready."

Dell reached his arm back inside. Marble's head bobbed as a contraction hit.

"Hang on, hang on," Dell said. "Come on, you ... Got 'im!"

Dell slowly pulled and his hand emerged with a horse's small hoof in it. "Now, tie it and hang on," Dell said.

Harrison slipped the rope around the hoof, keeping it in place against Dell's hand as he reached in for the second.

"This one's right here, right here..." Dell said.

Silvia hung on to Marble's neck with all her strength. The horse was pushing her against the wooden boards, crushing the breath out of her, but she didn't dare let go.

"Ok, slowly now, slowly ... pull with me!" Dell cried.

Dell's hand emerged with the second rear hoof, and Harrison pulled gently on the first one in unison. Marble convulsed and with a swooshing sound, the foal's back legs, chest, head, and finally, front legs tumbled out.

Harrison eased the colt to the ground and landed with a splat in the hay, coated with a gush of birthing water that the colt's breech position had been blocking. "Woo-hoo! I been baptized!!" he hollered.

Peter came in with the bucket of warm water, and the two men set to washing off the colt's face, opening its airway to breathe. Marble whinnied and shook her head. Silvia released her, and the mare turned and sniffed and licked her colt all over.

The black colt shook his head and they stepped back to watch in awe as it rose to its wobbly legs. Dell grabbed Silvia by the waist and spun her around.

"A colt! A beautiful star of a colt!" he yelled.

Silvia laughed, the exhilaration of the miraculous birth flooding through her. "I didn't know you could do such a thing!" she said. "You saved Marble and the colt!"

"I've seen it done, but never had to myself," Dell said, laughing and hugging her. "I couldn't have done it without you keeping Marble steady."

"What's all the ruckus?" a voice snickered from the barn hall. "You'd think a foal'd never been born before."

"Ralston! What the heck have you been doing around here while I was gone?" Dell's voice lowered to a deep growl. "I oughtta kill you for leaving Marble in her condition."

Silvia stepped back as the two men circled each other. Ralston's face sported a days'-old stubble, and his eyes were red and swollen. "Been takin' a holiday, just like you," he said. "Think you can keep me from my rightful place? I should'a gone to the stockyard sale with you, not this old washed-up has-been!"

Dell caught him by the collar and Ralston, in his condition, offered no resistance. Dell raised his right fist up high, ready to slam it into the sneering face.

"Dell, no!" Silvia cried. "Please — you're so happy Marble's all right, remember?"

Dell hesitated. Harrison stood up and came over to Silvia. "This is men's business, ma'am," he said.

"I don't care!" Silvia said. "Dell, let him go!"

Dell's blue eyes, gone black with rage, looked at Harrison. Harrison gave a slight shake of his head: No.

Dell's eyes shifted to Silvia. Her brown eyes and expectant face implored him to let Ralston go.

His eyes softened. He dropped the man to the floor. "Get out of my barn," Dell said. "Get off my ranch. And don't let me ever, ever catch you near here again."

Ralston crawled across the barn floor to put distance between him and Dell before shimmying to his feet. He stood a bit wobbly for a second and opened his mouth.

"You'll be sorry."

"Go!" Dell shouted.

Ralston turned on his heel and took off.

Chapter Fifteen

ilvia sipped the tea offered by Mrs. Magillan, trying to pull herself together. The excitement of the foal's birth and her respect for Dell swelled her heart with love. But the other side she had seen — Dell's rage and immediate impulse to fight — worried her mind.

"That no-good Ralston better not be back," Mrs. Magillan was saying.

"I'm not sure anyone would come around Dell after seeing that look in his eyes," Silvia said, shivering. "I'm not sure I'd want to."

"Mr. Casey has a bit of temper, yes," Mrs. Magillan said. "But he wouldn't hurt a woman, a horse, or a child. Nope. Never would."

Silvia stood wearily. "Thank you, Mrs. Magillan. I think it's time to go."

Allison and Peter were whispering together on the back porch. "I'll see you at the dance, then," Peter said. "We'll have the whole night together."

Allison didn't have the heart to tell him of her mother's plan for her and Dell. "I can't wait," she said.

Silvia came out of the kitchen. "Ready, Peter?"

"Yes. Good-bye, Allison."

"Good-bye," Allison said.

DELL CAME UP FROM THE BARN after making sure the colt was nursing well. He had cleaned out Marble's stall and gotten fresh hay, water, and feed for them. The yearlings' stalls needed cleaning as well, and he left Harrison to the work.

He came through the kitchen door. "Is Silvia still here?"

"No, sir," Mrs. Magillan said. Seeing the disappointment on his face, she continued. "I don't think you could've made her stay one second longer."

"What do you mean by that?"

"Well, it may not be my place, but you're my boss now. Mr. Casey, and I've got to tell you the truth. She was upset with you. Said she couldn't imagine being with a man with a temper like yours."

"She said that?" Dell couldn't believe it. Her face had been all smiles when he had let Ralston go. "She seemed fine with me out in the barn."

"Well, a woman may seem fine, but in here she poured out her heart," Mrs. Magillan turned up the drama. She had no problem promoting Allison as Dell's choice. If that meant a little exaggeration about Silvia's feelings, so be it.

"I'll never understand women," he said. "One minute they're smiling at you, and the next they're cutting you down." His face dropped.

Mrs. Magillan felt bad, but what was said was said. "Allison's plain with her feelings," she offered.

"Is she now?" Dell couldn't be bothered with any more woman talk. "I'm headed up to my room. And I don't want to be disturbed."

Chapter Sixteen

The next few days went by in a blur for Silvia. It was close to Nathalie's time to have her baby, and she depended on Silvia more to take over her work. Silvia couldn't get Dell off her mind. She had never seen a man so in love with a place and his work.

"Have a few minutes, dear?" Nathalie asked as the two friends sat in the parlor one morning. "Widow Garland is coming soon to check on me, and I thought you'd like to meet her. For when my time comes."

"Oh, I won't be much use to you. I was scared to death just watching Marble give birth! I can't imagine what help I can be."

"It's all right; I don't need you to attend the birth!" Nathalie said. "I'm scared myself. But Widow Garland is a fine midwife. She's talked me through it already; probably told me too much! Some of her counsel I don't really wish to know." She laughed nervously.

"If it's all the same to you, I'll mind the store. I want to go over the books with Peter again. I haven't quite gotten the hang of the bookkeeping yet."

"That's fine," Nathalie said, easing back on the couch. "I'll just keep resting, then."

Silvia gave Nathalie a kiss on the cheek. "I'd like to throttle that husband of yours," she said with a smile. "Imagine being gone with your wife in this condition!"

"Oh, he'll pay," Nathalie said. "He'll take the first week's night duty once the baby is here."

Nathalie thought for a minute, worried about her friend. She knew Silvia was interested in Dell, but she was holding back something.

"Make sure you close up early today. I want you to have plenty of time to get ready for the dance."

"I don't think I'll be going," Silvia said. "I don't want to leave you alone."

"Nonsense. Of course you're going! I'm not alone. I'll send Gadsen after you if anything happens. I want you to wear my green calico dress. It's upstairs in my trunk ... Oh!"

"What is it?" Silvia reached for her friend's hand.

"Oh!" Nathalie closed her eyes and breathed a few times. "There, it's stopped. It's nothing — yet. Widow Garland says these pains are just for practice. She'll let me know when things are close."

Silvia was relieved. The thought of Nathalie going into labor without Isadore home terrified her. She was not ready to be in charge of an emergency like that.

"Please don't worry about me," Nathalie said. "I'll be fine as long as you promise to go and have a good time. I believe Dell will be going, and you two need a chance to get to know each other better."

"All right. I promise," Silvia said. "But I think I know his type very well. Don't you know of any eligible preachers or undertakers or other peaceful men around here?"

Silvia giggled, and Nathalie laughed long and hard, holding her stomach.

THE ENTIRE TOWN AND HALF the county turned out for the dance. Peter was waiting to walk Silvia down the street to the hall.

"I know you'd rather be escorting Allison," Silvia said. "I'll try not to be in your way."

"I had planned to take her, but now Mr. Casey will be bringing her in to town," he said ruefully. "I don't know what she sees in me, but I hope it can survive living out there on the ranch with him."

Allison — and Dell? It hadn't occurred to Silvia that Allison was living on the ranch, with Dell. She knew the girl was working there ... Suddenly her stomach did a flip. Why had she not waited for Dell before she left? She wanted to tell him she was proud of him for not fighting with Ralston. Instead she had just left.

Silvia walked faster, more anxious than ever to see Dell.

The sound of music grew louder as they turned a corner and the church hall came into view. Horses and carts lined the street outside, and light and laughter poured out of the windows.

"There's Dell's buggy, come on!" Peter said. He rushed ahead into the hall.

Silvia hesitated a minute outside. She walked over to Harrison standing by the buggy.

"Aren't you going in?"

"Hello, Miss Silvia," Harrison smiled. "No, I won't be going in."

"Are you just going to stand out here all night?"

"Was thinking about it. I might sit for a spell."

Silvia laughed. "How's Marble and the little colt?"

"Alive and kicking," Harrison said. "Named him Thunderbolt, he's so fast. Marble's fine, like nothing ever happened. She keeps that colt close by, though. I think even she knows it was touch and go there for a minute."

"I'm sure she does," Silvia said. "I could — Harrison, I could see it in her eyes. She was scared and in pain, but when Dell talked to her ..."

"Yep. She trusts him. Once a horse trusts you, it's mighty hard to change their opinion."

Silvia was quiet, thinking of how she hadn't trusted Dell, even after how he had looked after her. Yet when she asked him not to beat Ralston, he had listened to her.

"Harrison, you thought Dell should have given Ralston a beating, didn't you?" she said.

"Yep. A man like that won't stop doin' wrong until somebody stops him. He was overdue for a lickin'."

"But fighting's never the best way, is it? I mean, I've seen terrible things come from fighting."

"It's like this. A good man doesn't love to fight. He fights because he loves something else, see?"

Silvia nodded her head. In the darkness, a tear rolled down from her eye. She sniffed.

"My Da loved me," she said and burst into tears.

"A' course he did," Harrison said, shifting from one foot to the other. "Now let's not have any more tears. Wipe your face. You got some dancin' to do."

Silvia took his handkerchief and wiped her eyes. She smiled at Harrison, reached up and kissed him on the cheek before turning and walking up to the door. She waved, and disappeared inside.

Chapter Seventeen

ilvia found Peter standing glumly against the wall, two cups of punch in his hands. She came up and he handed her a glass without taking his eyes off the dance floor. Silvia followed his gaze, and saw Allison's smiling face as Dell Casey twirled her around the floor.

"I'm too late," Peter said. "Look at how happy she looks!"

"I don't know," Silvia said. "I bet we can look happier together dancing. Come on!" She tugged on his hand.

They set down their cups and Peter took her in his arms. They swirled to the music around the wooden dance floor, getting closer and closer to Allison and Dell. Just as they came near, the song ended.

Allison clapped and smiled up at Dell. Peter walked up to her.

"Good evening, Allison," he said, and bowed. "Good evening, Mr. Casey."

"Peter! I've been wondering where you were!"

"Hmm, took a little longer to lock up the store tonight than I'd planned. May I have the next dance?" He looked at Allison's smiling face, and then at Dell.

"By all means," Dell said, and put Allison's hand in Peter's. He looked at Silvia, bowed, and walked away.

Silvia's smile fell from her face as she watched Dell's black hair and broad shoulders retreat through the waiting dancers. The music started, and without a partner, she crossed the dance floor to the other side by herself.

DELL SAW SILVIA SMILING at him, but scarcely trusted the look on her face. He could not be sure of her feelings.

Idiot! he thought as he marched away. *Running away will not spare my heart.* He roughly poured a glass of punch and downed it quickly. He took a chance to peruse the dance floor, expecting a hit to the gut upon seeing Silvia dancing with another man.

He could not find her dancing, and made his way around the perimeter of the room searching for her. When he spied her, he came up quietly behind her.

"Forgive me," he whispered.

"Oh!" Silvia jumped and turned, shock on her face to see him standing so close. "Dell, you startled me."

"I apologize for my behavior," Dell said.

"What?"

Dell cursed in frustration under his breath.

"Would you allow me to escort you outside?" he shouted over the music.

Silvia nodded yes, and put her hand on the bent arm he offered.

Outside, Dell shut the door behind him, glad of the chance to think clearly and impatient to find out what he wanted to know.

"How is Nathalie?"

"How is Marble?"

The questions came out at the same time.

They laughed nervously. They started again, saying in unison;

"Fine."

"Fine."

Silvia smiled and lowered her eyes.

Dell's agitation grew. He reached for her hand.

"Silvia," he said.

She looked up into his eyes, a worried look revealing itself from deep within.

"What is it? Dell?"

Dell searched her face for any sign. She looked at him with complete openness, brown eyes wide, clear skin and beautiful, full lips above her smooth, white neck. She moved a piece of her long, brown hair that had blown across her cheek.

"I must know, can you tell me honestly? Do you have any feelings for me? Before you answer, I will be as open as I can. Silvia, I love you. I've been miserable these few days without you, and I would have come calling right away if I hadn't thought ..."

"Thought what?" Silvia began to shake inside at the sound of the word 'love' falling from his lips.

"If I hadn't thought, no, was made to believe, that you would never have me." Dell finished.

Silvia wracked her mind wondering how he could think that. But she herself had been conflicted. Could she love him?

Maybe I already do.

"Dell, I've never been in love. I don't know what it feels like."

"It feels like thunderstorms and snowflakes," Dell said.

"Like train whistles and boat horns?"

"Yes — the excitement of movement, and motion — combined with a complete terror of not knowing."

"I've felt nothing but that since I met you," she said.

"So, could it be that you ... that you love me?"

Silvia smiled. "Yes. I do."

Dell grabbed her by the waist and spun her around, his joy uncontainable.

"Silvia! Be mine, then! Marry me. I only want to spend every day from this moment on with you!"

She wrapped her arms around his neck as he set her back on the ground. "Yes, Dell. I'll marry you."

He bent down and planted a gentle kiss on her lips. Silvia felt her heart would burst as she kissed him back, her fingers entwined in his hair, his hand supporting her back and holding her chin like a precious jewel.

Without warning, a horse and cart pulled up close, too close, to the loving couple. They jumped apart

Chapter Eighteen

r. Gadsen called down from the cart seat. "Silvia! Come quickly! Nathalie needs you!"

"Now?" Silvia asked. "Her time has come? Is Isadore back?"

"Yes, now! And no, Isadore telegraphed that his horse is lame. He'll come by train in the morning."

"Where is he?" Dell shouted. "I can take an extra horse and ride for him."

"Five miles south, from his last message," Gadsen said.

Dell turned to run for his horse, then stopped to kiss Silvia. "Be strong for her!" he said.

Silvia climbed up into the cart beside Mr. Gadsen. "I will! Be safe — and hurry!"

Gadsen slapped the horse's reins and pulled away. "We're stopping by to pick up Widow Garland," he said.

"Is Nathalie all right?"

"I think so — at least, she was when I left her. We were clearing up the supper table when I heard a crash. She dropped a plate right where she stood and went down on one knee. I got her up to her room, and Mrs. Gadsen helped her into bed. All I know is, when my wife came out, she told me to drive like the wind."

They pulled up in front of a house with a sign out front: "Garland Boarding House." Gadsen helped Silvia down from the cart and they rushed up the walk, rang the doorbell and knocked on the door.

The door opened and Silvia was about to ask for Widow Garland. A young woman not a few years older than she stood in the doorway. But Gadsen saw her and said two words: "Come, quickly!"

"Is her time come, so soon?" Widow Garland said. "She didn't seem this close earlier today. I'll get my things."

"I'm Silvia. Can I help you?"

Widow Garland smiled. "Nice to finally meet you, Silvia. Yes, come with me. Gadsen, can you turn the cart around? We'll be out in five minutes."

"Very nice to meet you," Silvia said. She followed Widow Garland into the front hall of her house. The hall opened to a large sitting room on one side, and a dining area with several tables and chairs on the other. Widow Garland turned out the lamp in the parlor, reached for her shawl and came back to the hall with a carpetbag. She set it on the table and rummaged around inside.

"Oh, I've left my sewing kit in my room at the top of the stairs," she said. "Can you fetch it for me? And turn out the light?"

Gadsen whistled from the street, and shouted, "I'm afraid there's not much time!"

"Yes, but please, go on ahead," Silvia said. "I know my way and I'll be right behind you."

"I suppose I won't need it until the end. Yes, I'm leaving now. Best I get there immediately. Thank you!"

She closed the door behind her and Silvia heard Gadsen say "Hiyah!" as they pulled away. She raced up the stairs and turned the knob of Widow Garland's bedroom door.

The room was large, with windows overlooking both the front and back of the house. It was simply furnished, with a large study area facing the street, a comfortable chair and sofa, and a bed on the back wall.

Silvia walked to the desk overlooking the street. Several books lay open and some papers and a writing pen where Widow Garland had left them. A photograph of a young man sat in a frame, his clear eyes looking out at her. A black ribbon draped across one corner.

Silvia saw a pouch on the edge of the desk, and opened it to find a neat sewing kit inside. She picked it up, turned — and heard a voice at the door. She knew that voice.

"Well, well." he said. "You're not Widow Garland."

Silvia turned to face Ralston blocking the door. She gasped and one hand covered her mouth.

Ralston laughed. "But I have seen you before. You saved me from a good whoopin'."

"Wh-what are you doing here?" Silvia stammered. She instinctively took a step back.

"Seems I live here, since the day I got kicked off the ranch," he said.

"I see. I'm glad you found a situation, then," Silvia said.

Ralston threw back his head and laughed. "I ain't 'found a situation,' thanks to Dell Casey," he said. "Unless I just found one right here."

"I must go," Silvia said and walked towards Ralston. "Let me pass."

"You're coming with me," Ralston said, his laughing face turning into a scowl. "And we'll see if Dell Casey changes his mind about me running the ranch."

Chapter Nineteen

ell and Isadore raced on their horses through the night. They rode too fast to talk, and there was nothing either man could say.

They rode into town a little after 2:00 a.m. The music in the church hall had gone quiet, and a few couples still strolled slowly home down the streets. They galloped on to the store. Isadore jumped off his horse and threw the reins to Dell.

"Can't thank you enough for coming after me," Isadore said. "If you don't mind, I'll be heading straight in."

"Go!" Dell said. "I'll look after the horses and come in to see if you need anything."

Inside the house, Mr. Gadsen paced the floor. Mrs. Gadsen heard her son's footsteps on the porch. "He's come," she said.

Mr. Gadsen stopped as Isadore came bursting through the door. "Mother! Gadsen! How is she?"

"You'll have to find out and tell us," Mr. Gadsen said. "Widow Garland is with her. It's been awful quiet this last hour."

Isadore kissed his mother. "Go to her, son," she said.

In two long paces he was at the stairs, and disappeared up to their bedroom.

Dell came in shortly after. "Any news?" he asked the couple.

"None from Nathalie — thank goodness you were able to get Isadore," Mr. Gadsen said. "But we haven't seen Silvia since I left her at Widow Garland's a couple of hours ago."

"Silvia! Why did you leave her? Have you looked for her?"

"I'm sorry, Mr. Casey. She stayed behind to bring some extra things for Widow Garland. When she didn't come along right away, your friend, Harrison, went after her."

"Good," Dell said. "I better go see what's up." Dell left, retrieved his tired horse, and headed through town to Widow Garland's.

He arrived to find the front door wide open. He walked in and found two men sitting at the dining tables with a piece of paper lying on the table between them.

"Gentlemen: Name's Dell Casey. Either of you seen my man, Harrison? Or a brown-haired woman about this tall?" Dell raised his hand to his shoulder height.

"No, sir. Ain't nobody here. We got home from the dance a little while ago, and ain't seen the Widow Garland, either. Found her door open upstairs and this note on it." The man held up the piece of paper.

Dell crossed to the table and took the note out of the man's hand.

Dell read it out loud: You can have either the girl or the ranch, but not both. –R.J.

His eyes turned to slivers as he clenched his fist. The two men at the table cowered in their seats.

Dell kept reading. Underneath in a different hand, it said: Over my dead body. Gone to get her back. –H

A twisted grin came over Dell's face. Harrison was on their trail. Now he just had to track Harrison.

DELL DROPPED THE PAPER and traipsed through to the back of the house in search of a lantern. He came out with it, lit a taper from the candle on the table, lit the lantern, and headed into the night without a word.

He went back out to the street and examined the dirt. He saw that a set of wagon wheel tracks had made a circle in the street. Gadsden's cart. He found a deep set of tracks where someone had spurred his horse down the street away from town. That'd be Harrison. He held the lantern up high to the right and left when he saw something flapping on the fence. He walked over to it and pulled it loose.

His handkerchief. The one he had given Silvia back in Sioux Falls. He smiled to himself. She was alert enough to try to leave him a clue. With only one set of tracks heading away from town, he reasoned Ralston had her on foot. They couldn't have gotten far before Harrison overtook them. He took off in the direction of Harrison's horse.

Dell rode slowly, holding the lantern low and peering down at the tracks he was following. He soon realized he was heading back to Eagle River Ranch. He reached forward and talked to his horse, "Just a couple more miles, Dusty," he whispered. Then he kicked his heels into his sides.

HARRISON WASN'T NEARLY AS GOOD a tracker as Dell, and at first he thought he would easily overcome Ralston and Silvia by following their footsteps. He lost the tracks, though, and started following a set of cart tracks instead. When he got to the end of the lane leading to the ranch, he walked his horse in the rest of the way.

An unfamiliar horse and wagon stood in front of the house. That rascal adds thievin' to his crimes, he thought.

A single light shown from a front window. Harrison crept up the porch steps, crawled to the window and looked inside. Mrs. Magillan's back was to him, the large woman sitting straight in a chair in her nightdress and nightcap. Ralston paced the room, talking loudly.

"And when he comes, I don't want a peep out of you! It's time we had a man-to-man talk about the ranch. Uncle Julius should have known I'm the better man to carry on the family name. That Casey line is not even blood! They say his father was part Injun ..."

"His father was British, Ralston, you know that," Mrs. Magillan said.

"I don't care! I'm the son of his brother! Blood is blood!" he continued to rant.

Where is Silvia? Harrison wondered. He didn't see her as he scanned the room. He crept off the porch and went around back to peer in the kitchen windows. All was dark and quiet. He stood and pushed his hat back to scratch his head.

Neeeiigghh!!!

Marble!

Harrison raced over to the barn and opened the door. The horses were quiet in their stalls, standing and lying down, asleep. He left the door open so the light of the moon fell in softly. Marble stuck her nose out of the last stall and whinnied to him.

Harrison was at her side in a moment, checking her over. She was fine, but nervous. She bobbed her head up and down, neighing and whinnying.

"Shh ... quiet now, girl. I'm here and I'm listening. Where is she? Have you seen Silvia?"

A muffled sound came from the large birthing stall, which had been padlocked shut. Harrison climbed the door and looked down inside.

Silvia lay on her side, hands tied behind her back and a cloth covering her mouth. Little Thunderbolt was in the stall, dancing in front of her and pushing at her with his nose.

In an instant, Harrison climbed up over the door and jumped down on the hay beside her. He uncovered her mouth and her brown eyes looked up at him.

"Harrison! Thank goodness! He's crazy, that one! He's in the house, waiting for Dell!"

"I know, honey," Harrison said as he loosened the rope around her hands. "Let me get you out of here and I'll take care of that varmint."

The padlock jangled and someone opened the stall door. "Well, now, ain't this nice? You've got company, little lady," Ralston said.

He held a lantern high and Silvia was terrified by the wild look in his eyes.

Harrison rushed at him and the two wrestled across the barn floor, the lantern fallen to the ground.

Silvia struggled in her loosened ropes but couldn't get her hands free. "Help! Help!" she yelled, but there was no one to hear.

Chapter Twenty

*L*ittle Thunderbolt pranced around Silvia, excited by her yelling and the two men rolling in the barn. Silvia turned her back to him and leaned into him. He nipped and nibbled at her dress. She bent forward and pushed her elbows up to get the ropes nearer to his mouth.

"Ouch!" She yelled as Thunderbolt nipped her arm. "A little lower, just grab the rope!"

Harrison was on his back as Ralston grabbed for his throat. He coughed and wheezed as the younger man choked the breath out of him. He could see the lamp was overturned on a bare patch of dirt. The idea that this crazy fool had tied up Silvia and was fool enough to put the horses in danger enraged him. He brought his arms up underneath Ralston's elbows and pushed out as hard as he could. Ralston's grip broke and Harrison flipped him over onto his back, jumped on his stomach and pounded his face.

"Stop! That's enough, Harrison!" Silvia said. She stood holding the lantern high, rope still trailing off one arm. "Let him up."

Harrison looked at Ralston's bloody nose and gave him one more tap. He climbed off him and hauled the man up by one arm.

Ralston stood, breathing heavily. "Thank you," he said to Silvia. Then he threw an elbow into Harrison's stomach. The older man's grip broke as he fell to his knees.

Silvia screamed and ran at Ralston. He grabbed her wrists and laughed as she tried to pummel him. "I'll thank you to stay where you're put. My business ain't with you, unless Dell chooses the ranch. Then you're mine."

A shot rang out. Dell stood in the doorway of the barn.

"That was your warning," he said, pulling the barrel of the rifle down and pointing it at Ralston. "Let her go."

Ralston didn't turn around. He let Silvia go, and grabbed the lantern, holding it up high as he swung to face Dell. Silvia rushed to Harrison's side, helping him up. "I'm sorry," she said.

"Hmmph."

"You want me," Dell said. "Let them and the animals go. We'll talk."

"We're done talkin'," Ralston said. "That piece of paper you call a will ain't going to ruin my life. You got a choice. Either sign the ranch over to me, or the barn goes up in flames."

"You won't do it, if you claim to love these horses."

"Better they're all dead, and you have to start over like I do."

The two men stood glaring at each other.

"You said it was a choice," Silvia said. "Take me instead."

"Silvia, no!" Dell shouted.

She walked toward Ralston. "I'll go with you. I won't try to run."

Ralston kept his eyes on Dell. He smiled, then lunged toward Silvia. Grabbing her shoulder, he spun her around and held his arm against her neck, her body pulled tight against him.

Dell kept the rifle pointed at Ralston and marched forward into the barn. "Let her go, now! Or I'll blow your head off."

"Or hers, eh?" Ralston laughed. "Sure you're that good a shot?"

The two men's eyes locked. Harrison shimmied across the barn floor.

Dell took a step forward.

Ralston pulled Silvia a step backward. "Which is it then, Dell? I wouldn't mind a wife like her. Kinda feisty! And pretty, to boot."

Dell made a low sound deep in his throat. His eyes glinted in the light of the lantern that Ralston still held high. He moved the barrel of the rifle, and fired.

The lantern flew out of Ralston's hand and hit the ground. He took a step back and tripped over Harrison, crouched on the floor behind him. Silvia spun free and stomped out the flame before it could spread.

Dell was on Ralston in a second. He raised his fist and looked at Silvia.

She nodded her head. Yes.

The energy and fear that ran through Dell came down in the force of one blow. Ralston lay limp at his feet.

"Nice shot," Harrison said.

Dell let out a loud breath. "I figured at least if I missed the lantern, I wouldn't hit Silvia.

"I meant your knockout punch," Harrison said, kneeling on the ground and smiling down at Ralston's crumpled body. "Course, I wore him down a bit before you made your appearance."

Dell threw back his head and laughed along with Harrison.

Silvia rushed into Dell's arms. "I knew you'd come!" She stood on her tiptoes and pressed kisses into his cheeks.

"Hold on, hold on there! Are you all right? Did he hurt you?"

"No, I kept my distance. Told him you never know what kind of disease I might be carrying from the crowded tenements of New York!"

"Smart girl!" Dell said.

"Disease? What's that you say?" Harrison said in mock horror. Dell and Silvia looked at him and broke into laughter as a wide smile spread across his face.

Chapter Twenty-one

"I've got to hand it to you," Mrs. Magillan said as Silvia finished the embroidery in her apron. "I've always had a soft spot for knitting and lace, but seeing what you can do with a bit of floss is inspiring, indeed it is."

"Thank you! I'd be glad to teach you," Silvia said. She looked around the kitchen, amazed at the pans on the stove, the white dishes stacked on open shelves, and the crocks of butter, coffee, flour and sugar lining the pantry. In the last week since moving to the ranch, it already felt like home.

"Achh, the work's too fine for my eyes at this age. Maybe Allison would like to learn."

"Sure, I could show her during slow times at the store. I hope you don't mind that she decided to move back to town and take my place."

"It's for the best. It took a bit of air out of my sister, that it did. But I have a feeling Allison will learn to work a little, which her mother had to agree never hurt anyone. But as for these *kolache*, as you call them," Mrs. Magillan paused as she huffed over pulling a sheet pan out of the large iron stove, "these little darlings are going right into my baking schedule. There!"

Silvia's nose was filled with the scent of the warm pastries as Mrs. Magillan proudly bustled around. She smiled at the round forms, some filled with plum jam and others with soft white cheese. She hadn't yet acquired the poppy seed she needed for her favorite with walnuts, but soon Nathalie would carry it at the store.

She was glad Allison would be able to spend more time with Peter. She knew Nathalie was concerned that Peter wouldn't be able to keep his mind on his work, but Peter had taken on a bigger role since

Nathalie's baby was born and he was all business.

Silvia smiled at the thought of little Nathan. She would still be helping Nathalie with him as much as she could, and she was smitten with the baby.

"You ladies are going to spoil me with all these treats," Dell said as he came in to the kitchen.

Silvia quickly pulled the apron she was stitching under the table. "Good morning! You've slept in a bit today."

He came over and gave her a kiss on the hair.

"Not true, my love. I've been out to the barn and back already. Was just catching up on my work in the office until the baking smells got to my stomach." He smiled at Mrs. Magillan.

"You can have one, but these are for the wedding guests tomorrow! And don't be surprising us after this! You can't be seeing Silvia for the rest of the day, now! It would bring bad luck."

"I'll stay out of your way and not vex the leprechauns," Dell said mischievously.

Mrs. Magillan flapped a towel at him. "Go on, then. Take one and go!"

Dell grabbed a *kolach* and bowed, backing his way through the door to the dining room.

Silvia laughed. She was nervous about the guests coming to Eagle River Ranch for the wedding, but Mrs. Magillan had everything in hand. Mr. Gadsen had promised to come this afternoon to help set up the parlor and put out the dishes and silverware.

"Will Widow Garland be coming, do you think?" Silvia asked.

"Now that, I don't know. She might have another birth to attend or she might just not be ready."

"I hope she will. I know how much Dell and Isadore think of her, after she brought Nathan into the world. Why doesn't she get remarried? Why do they call her 'Widow Garland' when she is so young?"

"They've respected her long before Nathan was born," Mrs. Magillan said, shaking her head. "We all do. 'Tis a sad tale, that it is. Her husband, Cap Garland, God rest his soul, was a type we'll not soon see again. I'll tell you the story one of these days, dear. I've got to get the wet linens out on the line, now. There's so much to do!"

Silvia nodded, her heart drawn to the woman who had taken the time the night of

Nathan's birth to help Silvia clean up her cuts and scrapes from her encounter with Ralston. She thought of the black-ribbon draped picture of the man on the widow's desk – his eyes haunting her. She bent her head over and finished the last section of stitches on her wedding apron.

THE NEXT MORNING, Silvia taught Mrs. Magillan how to help her into her *kroj*.

"Now stuff a bit more crinolin up into my sleeve," Silvia told Mrs. Magillan. "That's it, bigger!"

"These sleeves are bigger than you are!" she answered. "Now, let me tie on this sash."

Silvia turned around and smiled at herself in the full-length mirror in her large room. Her mother would be so happy to know she was wearing the traditional *kroj* dress for her wedding. And Da would be downstairs, having a drink with Dell and all his relatives before they all walked to the church.

But this was the Eagle River Ranch, and their friends were coming here for the wedding.

Mrs. Magillan took the long, wide ribbon and centered it across Silvia's middle before pulling the ends to the back. She worked at the beautiful material, pulling it into a wide bow that covered Silvia from side-to-side.

"Can you make sure the ends are even with the edge of the skirt?" Silvia asked. "My mother always made sure they were just so."

"I can see that, darlin'" Mrs. Magillan said. "It looks beautiful."

Silvia turned to the side and inspected what she could see of the bow. A big smile crossed her face and she hugged the older woman.

"My apron, now, can you help? I don't want to wrinkle these sleeves!"

Mrs. Magillan handed Silvia the apron, and Silvia reached the ends of it behind her so they could be tucked in out of sight. She beamed.

Nathalie smiled from the bed, where she sat holding her month-old boy. "Nathan thinks you're the most beautiful bride he's ever seen," she said.

Silvia kissed the baby and hugged Nathalie, a tear of joy in her eye.

Nathalie stood and handed the baby to Mrs. Magillan, who took him downstairs with her. "Are you ready? Stay right behind me, but wait at the top of the stairs until I'm at the bottom," she said. "I want all eyes to be on you."

Silvia nodded.

Chapter Twenty-two

ell took his place in front of the fireplace with Harrison at his side. The old man fidgeted and bounced.

"Stay still, man, you're making me more nervous than I already am!" Dell said.

"Can't help it, these clothes itch worse than sleeping in a briar patch."

"Well hang on, this will be over soon."

"That's what you think," Harrison grumbled.

Dell elbowed him as they heard Nathalie's footsteps coming down the stairs and watched her take her place next to Isadore. Silvia must be ready.

She appeared, holding the banister to steady herself, and smiled at all her friends in the room. She couldn't see through to the fireplace where Dell was waiting for her, but she could see Isadore standing tall, eyes shining. and Mr. and Mrs. Gadsen seated in a place of honor. Mrs. Simms, Allison and Peter sat across from them, and other friends of Dell's and Nathalie's filled the room. Widow Garland sat by herself. Silvia sighed, thinking of her Mother and dear Da.

If only Emil were here.

Silvia stood at the top of the stairs and waited. The organ music changed to the wedding march.

Dell stopped poking Harrison and stood still as a statue. His heart was in his throat as he worried for a moment that Silvia was not coming downstairs. The room was still.

A dark shoe appeared followed by a slim leg in white stockings. Soon Silvia was halfway down the staircase, resplendent in her handmade dress with its multicolored flowers embroidered on the red skirt and apron, beautiful yellow sash, figure-hugging vest and brilliant white, embroidered sleeves framing her smiling face. A garland of wildflowers encircled her head.

She walked to Dell's side and took his hand. The music ended and Parson Brown said a few words.

"We are gathered here today to join this man, Dell Casey, and this woman, Silvia Johnson, in holy matrimony. If any man has cause to prevent this union, let him speak now or forever hold his peace."

Silvia quietly waited. Dell glanced at Harrison. He opened his mouth as if to speak – then smiled at Dell and chuckled.

"Good," Parson Brown said, looking sternly over his glasses at Harrison. "Before we begin, I have a letter entrusted to me from the bride's brother. He asked that I read it to you all now."

Silvia gasped. She had known it would not be possible for Emil to come to her wedding. She didn't know that when he sent his reply, he had sent a separate letter for Nathalie to give the parson.

The parson read:

> *I greet you all on this joyous day for Silvia and Dell. I wish I was there to celebrate with you. For this occasion,*

I ask two things to seal the bond according to the traditions of my family.

First, may the loving couple eat their first meal from the same dish, to signify how they will need to share and work together to have a happy life.

Second, I ask that the women there help Silvia to put on this bonnet made by our Aunt Patsy. It signifies her becoming a wife, and will mean a great deal to us in memory of our dear Mother and Father.

With love and best wishes,

Emil Johnson

Everyone smiled and nodded at such a warm greeting from the bride's brother. Silvia looked at Nathalie, who showed her the lovely handmade bonnet Emil had sent.

She smiled up at Dell.

"Ahem, let us continue. Do you, Dell Casey, take Silvia Johnson to be your lawfully wedded wife? Do you promise to love her and honor her, in sickness and in health, as long as you both shall live?"

"I do." Dell said. He took a ring from his pocket and held it to Silvia's finger. "With this ring, I pledge thee my troth," he said as he slipped the ring onto her finger.

"And do you, Silvia Johnson, take this man, Dell Casey, to be your lawfully wedded husband? Do you promise to love, honor and obey him, in sickness and in health, as long as you both shall live?"

"I do," Silvia said. She held Dell's hand with shaking fingers and slipped a gold ring onto his. "With this ring, I pledge thee my troth." She looked in Dell's eyes and felt her heart soar.

"Obey?" she heard Harrison mutter under his breath. "Not likely."

Dell stepped backwards onto his foot, hard, knowing Harrison would not be able to yell out.

"In the name of God and in sight of this crowd of witnesses, I pronounce you Husband and Wife," said the parson.

Dell caught Silvia close to him and she bent her face up toward him. They stood locked in a loving embrace and kissed each other.

"Ahem – yes, well, you may kiss the bride!"

Everyone clapped and cheered. Little Nathan stirred awake and started to cry. Nathalie bounced him on her shoulder and hugged him close.

"Shh, I know, quiet now," Nathalie whispered to him, tears streaming down her face. "I'm crying with you, dearest one!"

About the Author

*L*orena Dove has been reading and dreaming about living during the great westward migration since she was a young child growing up in New York and then Virginia. A descendent of Italian and German immigrants, she enjoys the interplay of cultures and passing down of traditions, recipes and family values to her children and grandchildren.

Lorena raised four children in a modernized 1880s log cabin for 10 years in West Virginia. The seasons of nature, the beauty of the mountains and rivers, and the simple enjoyment of gardening, reading and quilting have been her passions.

She lives with her husband, a retired Marine Corps colonel, and sons in Virginia. She collaborates on books with her daughter, whose passion for historical fiction exceeds her own, and is waiting for her granddaughters to fit into their mother's dress-up hoopskirts and bonnets.

You can keep in touch with Lorena by visiting her on Facebook at LorenaDoveBooks, or sign up for her VIP Readers Group at LorenaDove.com.

More Books in the Sweet Land of Liberty Brides Series

Book 1: *Giovanna*: *The Cowboy's Calabrese Mail Order Bride* ~ Can a young Italian widow win the love of a Nordic cowboy in time to save the only thing she loves?

Book 2: **Nathalie**: *The Circuit Rider's Rhineland Mail Order Bride* ~ Can practical Nathalie find love in the strong arms of an intellectual dreamer?

Book 3: *Silvia*: *The Stockman's Slovak Mail Order Bride* ~ Silvia flees a violent past and heads to the west hoping for safety and dreaming of love. Can Dell, a 'Black Irish' stockman and reformed fighter, win her heart if he must fight for it?

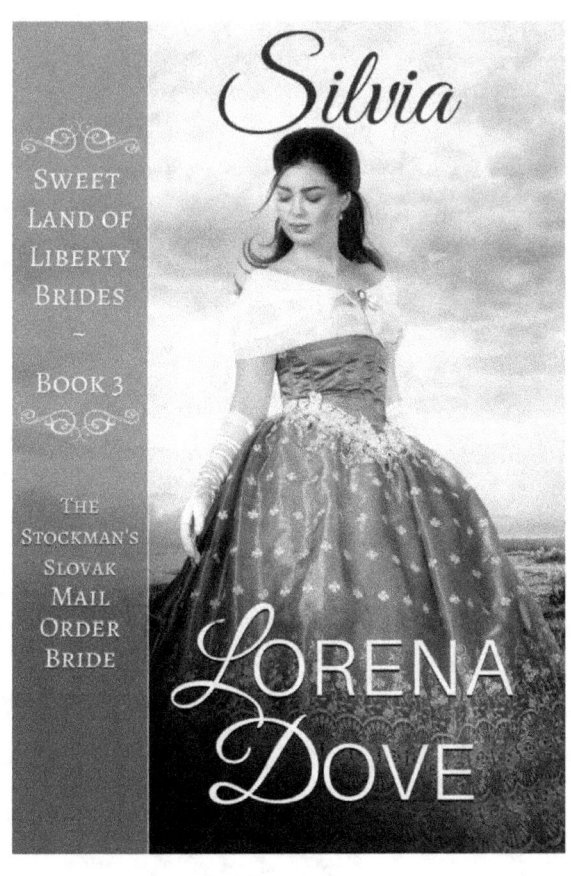

Book 4: Louisa: *Cap Garland's Irish Mail Order Bride ~*
` Read below for a free sample of ***Louisa.***

Louisa:

Cap Garland's Irish Mail Order Bride

"Don't worry now, Silvia, you're young and strong and your baby is going to be fine."

"If I could only breathe a little easier – and bend over to lace my shoes!" Silvia laughed, but her shortness of breath made it sound more like wheezing.

Louisa Garland laughed with her. "You're carrying a bit high still. Don't worry; as you get closer to your time, the baby will drop.

You'll be able to breathe a little easier, but then you'll have a few new problems."

"I can't wait to find out," Silvia said, shaking her head. "And to think after all this, women go ahead and have more babies!"

"The nine months prepare you for the birth," said Louisa, smiling softly. "When it's time, you'll go through whatever you have to for the baby to be born. My only concern right now is that I can feel the baby's feet and legs down low where its head should be. But there's plenty of time for it to turn."

"You mean the baby is breach?" Siliva's hand flew up to her mouth. The image of Dell pulling [Snowball's) foal out with a rope tied around its legs filled her mind. Best he didn't hear anything about the possibility. She wouldn't let him within 10 feet of her with a rope.

Dell Casey knocked on the door.

"All finished, ladies?"

"Yes, Dell," Silvia called to her husband. To Louisa, she pleaded: "Not a word."

Louisa nodded her head in agreement. *There I go opening my mouth again*, she thought. *When will I learn to keep some things to myself?*

Dell cracked the door and his blue eyes crinkled from beneath his black eyebrows. He scanned the room mischievously. "Is it safe to come in?"

"Nothing more gruesome to see than my rather swollen self!"

Dell swung the door open, and stood with his hands on his hips. He smiled appreciatively at Silvia as she stood near the bed adjusting her skirts and trying to smooth her apron over her round midsection. "You're beautiful, darling, and don't you forget it! Well, how long will it be, do you think?"

"A few more weeks, at least," Louisa said. "Definitely before the snow flies, if the weather holds."

Allison Simms stood by the ironing board, pressing baby clothes, folding them, and putting them away in a small chest of drawers. Louisa turned to her.

"If you're finished, we'd best be getting back to town," she said, putting the last of her things in her carpet bag.

"I'm on the last one," Allison said, straightening out a tiny infant gown. "These are so adorable! Silvia, come see the sweet bow on this one."

Silvia and Allison giggled and discussed for the hundredth time whether the baby would be a girl or a boy. Louisa snapped closed her bag.

"Here, let me help you with that," Dell said.

Louisa had already hoisted the bag and was headed toward the door. "I can carry it. I'll be waiting in the buggy, Allison."

Dell followed the Widow Garland down the stairs and out to the horse and buggy he had brought around for her. He stood uselessly as she placed the heavy bag up onto the floorboards, grabbed the side handle, and pulled herself up into the driver's seat. Just as she reached for the reigns he had laid across the bench, they slipped through behind the horse's tail.

"Here, I can least save you from climbing back down," Dell said. "Or do you not want my help at all?"

Louisa looked at him sharply before seeing the grin on Dell's face. "I'd be much obliged," she said.

Dell handed her the reigns. "Seriously, you'd tell me if there's something I need to do for Siliva, wouldn't you? I just want to make sure I take care of her until her time comes."

Louisa looked into the face turned up toward her, the face of a man who wanted to fix things, and to know what his chances were. A look of determination and self-assurance, so much like Ed's and most of the good men she had known.

"You're doing everything you can for her right now," Louisa said. "Keep her spirits up, make sure she eats well and rests. Tell her she's beautiful, because that's the only thing she doesn't believe right now."

Dell smiled and turned toward the sound of Allison and Silvia coming onto the porch. The two women hugged, and Dell went around to help Allison up into the other side of the buggy.

"Thank-you, Dell. Good-bye, Silvia! Good-bye!" she waved and called as Louisa slapped the reigns and the buggy and headed off in autumn's afternoon sun.

"I'm so glad you asked me to come with you today!" Allison said. "I thought it would make Silvia nervous, having me there while you examined her."

"Somehow being pregnant strips away a bit of a woman's embarrassment," Louisa said. "You become used to being poked and prodded, and you're just thinking of the health of the baby. Besides, now that she's further along, I wanted to find out if you would be interested in helping out when her time comes."

"Me? Really? I guess so, I mean, do you think I'd be any use? I haven't learned much about birthing yet."

"You'd be surprised how useful an extra pair of hands can be," Louisa said. "I prefer not to rely on the husbands at such times. Doing that does seem to make the mother nervous. I'll definitely need you if the baby remains in the breech position."

"If you're sure," Allison said. "I wish I were as certain as you." Allison rode along in silence. "I'm scared thinking about it now; what if I just freeze when you really need my help?"

"You won't. Between now and the delivery, I'll tell you everything I expect to happen, and what kind of things you may need to do. You're a steady girl, Allison, and smart. Of course, I'm assuming a lot. Do you have an interest in learning about childbirth?"

Allison giggled to cover her embarrassment. "Childbirth! It seems like there would be so much to learn. I do hope to go on in school and become a teacher.

Mother has hopes for me to attend the Methodist Teacher's College. I don't know. I would have to go so far away."

"I was studying to be a teacher, too. Becoming a midwife just seemed like another way to use my talents."

"Did your husband approve, though? I would think a man wouldn't want his wife travelling all over the territory."

Louisa's eyes scanned the horizon as she smiled. "He did. Edmond encouraged me, in fact." She slowed the horse by pulling gently on the reins. "There; I knew we were close."

Allison looked in the direction of Louisa's gaze at the broad swaths of brown grass waving across the open plains. "There— what?"

"Do you mind if we take a little detour? I want to show you something."

Allison nodded, and Louisa directed the horse toward an overgrown path on one side of the road. She headed across the prairie to a stand of trees and an abandoned shanty. Allison bumped and jostled along beside her, holding onto the side rail and wondering where they were going.

Louisa pulled the horse up in front of the shanty and climbed down. Allison scrambled down after her. Louisa walked around back of the shanty and returned to the front. She rested her hand on the trunk of a tree.

"Was this your place—yours and Mr. Garland's?"

"Yes. Edmond and I called this home."

Allison looked at the tall Widow Garland and saw a change wash over the older woman. Louisa's face grew soft and her mouth turned up at the corners in a wry grin. She took off her bonnet and pulled the pin out of her bun, letting her long auburn hair fall down. She shook her head and the breeze whipped at her hair. She let out a long breath and spread her arms out wide, moving her feet in a slow circle. The years seemed to melt off her face. She was only 31, but carried herself with the demeanor and burden of a much older woman.

Allison should have been embarrassed to see Widow Garland in such an unguarded state, but her curiosity at the change in Louisa captivated her as she sat beneath the tree and waited.

Louisa breathed in the air and felt as if her lungs could not hold enough of it. As she stood at the place where she last saw Edmond alive, she felt as if his energy and love was flowing through her, up from the warm ground and around her in the blowing wind. She wanted to take it in, to take him in. After years of closing off the pain, she now wanted to embrace it and feel it. She turned in slow circles, her arms outstretched, and gloried in the life she had lost.

Tears came to her eyes and she let them fall. She wasn't sad any more. She was alive, and she had loved and been loved. Her heart jumped as she remembered Cap's face close to her, the smell of his hair, their bodies entwined. Cap was all around her in this same waving grass and forever sky.

After a few minutes, she gathered her hair and smoothed it behind her back. She looked at Allison's awed face, her eyes smiling.

"I'm sorry, I didn't know I would feel like this."

"Are you all right?"

"Yes. I'm all right. And that's a marvelous thing."

Allison's eyes looked more puzzled then before. "I don't understand."

Louisa lifted her skirts and settled down in the grass next to Allison, leaning against the tree. The bumps of the craggy bark pressed against her back, at once grounding her to the pain and steeling her to reliving the heartaches.

"I've been afraid to come here. Afraid I would sink back into the pit of sadness I lived through after Edmond's death. But that's the amazing thing! I am sad, but I did live through it. People told me at the time that I would; I just couldn't believe it."

Allison nodded slowly, pretending to understand. "I'm sure I wouldn't know how I'd live through losing my husband so young, assuming I'll ever have a husband."

"Oh, you will!" Louisa said. "It did help having this calling. It's hard to be sad all the time when you're helping bring new life into the world. I am fortunate to have had the training; I didn't know how much I would have to depend on it."

"How did you learn? It must have taken an awful long time. You're young, for a midwife."

"Yes, that's what the husbands used to say!" Louisa laughed. "I was just about your age when I found myself working at the side of a midwife. It certainly wasn't by choice, and I didn't really have any notice. But I was determined that Cap Garland's child would come into the world safely."

"His baby! You mean, yours and his? I didn't know you had children!" Allison looked around, as if she could find a child hiding somewhere on the claim.

Pick up your copy of **Louisa** today to read her full story, how she came to be a midwife and marry Cap Garland, and how she finds love again 10 years after his untimely death.

ALSO BY LRENA DOVE

Mail Order Bride: Saved by Grace,~ Fraternal twins, Annabelle and Willie, whose widowed father is about to remarry, send for a mail-order bride to prevent him marrying a woman they hate. Can Grace Haggerty overcome her embarrassment that Will does not want her for a wife?

Mail Order Bride: Celia's Secret Baby, Book 7 in the Blessed with Babies multi-author series from the Clean & Wholesome Book Club ~ Abandoned as a child, Celia determines to carry on with her plan to be a mail order bride even after the death of her best friend at the orphanage. Thomas is still under the thumb of a sister who is trying to run his life. Can Thomas forgive Celia for keeping something so secret as a baby—one she had given his name?

Mail Order Bride: Angie's Hope, Book 7 in the Valentine's Day Mail Order Brides series from the Clean & Wholesome Book Club ~ Angie is ready for her engagement to expire when she meets and falls in love with Cal. But her brother in Kansas City now has different plans for her that don't include Cal. Can Angie marry the man who truly loves her before it's too late?

Christmas Bride: Susan's Secret Baby ~ A widow with a secret heads to the Oklahoma Territories as a possible wife for a lonely farmer with three children.

Find these and all new releases by Lorena Dove on Amazon, or visit

http://www.LorenaDove.com

http://www.Facebook.com/LorenaDoveBooks